Authored and Photographed by Wong How Man

CULTURE MY DESTINY

文化
志向

黃效文 —— 著

序

摯友黃效文兄出版自然文化新書二冊，囑咐小弟撰寫序言。小弟久未執筆，不知從何寫起，自己在問，究竟如何初次認識效文？腦波頻動，立時走進時光隧道。

時維一九九九年，正值金秋，邀得黃效文兄替小弟公司拍攝數碼攝錄機電視廣告宣傳片，故事內容簡潔，展示此激情探險家喜愛備帶 Panasonic 數碼攝錄機，周遊歷險，紀錄澎湃江河、崇山峻嶺、壯觀原野等景象。十分肯定，從此以後，吾兄一直使用著小弟代理品牌之攝錄機、電飯煲、手提電話、冷氣機、雪櫃等等，不一而足。如今吾兄府上，眾多工作據點，誠像小弟代理品牌之產品陳列室也。

效文兄乃吾一生之中遇見以探險事業為生第一人，絕非兒時所閱歷險故事所述泛泛之輩。探索奇峰異洞、涉獵名山大川、駕馭越野戰車、馳騁於密林沙漠之間之一般探險家歷練，吾兄定必經歷無數。

當吾隨效文兄造訪其重建之修道院，方知吾兄一以探險，

FOREWORD

When How Man asked me to write a foreword for his two new books, I asked myself, "When did I first meet How Man? How did I get to know him?" My memory immediately went through the time tunnel; it was sometime in the fall of 1999. My company wanted to ask him to help promote on TV a product that he has been using in rather extreme conditions in the field. The storyline was very simple. It was about this very passionate explorer, Wong How Man, who loved to use a Panasonic Movie Camera.

I am pretty sure that it was from that moment onward that How Man started to use my movie cameras, my rice cookers, my mobile phones, my air conditioners, my refrigerators, etc., etc., And now, his homes and all his sites look just like my showrooms.

For me, it was my first time to encounter a person who made his career in exploration. How Man is not the usual explorer that I read about in story books when I was a kid. Of course, I am sure that he has crawled inside many caves, climbed many mountains and sped his Land Rover through many jungles and deserts. When he took me to the nunnery that he restored, however, I was

一以復修；當吾手抱效文兄試從英國帶回緬甸之緬甸貓，方才得知吾兄尚且保育稀有品種動物；當吾見證效文兄引薦二位來自古巴老婦，詠唱粵曲於香港石澳文物古屋之中，吾對效文兄工作所觸及領域之廣闊，甚感嘆為觀止。效文兄尋幽訪勝，時有驚人發現，每每給人帶來意外驚喜。

效文吾兄，擇善固執，探險精神，堅持不渝！小弟樂於偶爾奉陪，攜手踏上征途。

蒙德揚

中國探險學會 董事會成員
二零一六年十月

Mr. David Mong with Burmese kittens / 蒙德揚先生與緬甸幼貓

amazed that he not only explored, he also restored. When I held those Burmese Cats that he purchased from the United Kingdom, I then learned that he was preserving this endangered breed and was bringing them back home to Burma. When I saw the Chinese Opera performance by the two old Cuban ladies in Shek O, I was stunned once again by the scope of work of How Man.

Wong How Man always surprises me with his new "findings". Keep up with the good work pal. I promise that I will join you on expedition again soon.

David Mong

Member of the Board
China Exploration and Research Society
October 2016

JACK YOUNG, A CENTENARIAN CHINESE PILOT AT 101

JACK YOUNG，一百零一歲的中國飛行員―――010

PILGRIMAGE LONG OVERDUE

姍姍來遲的朝聖―――032

REMEMBERING HISTORY, SEVENTY YEARS AGO

回憶七十年前的歷史―――054

SHADOW OF GEORGE ORWELL'S BURMESE DAYS

喬治・歐威爾在緬甸日子下的影子―――070

LOTUS SCARF - from the house of Nang

蓮花絲巾，在 *Nang* 的家中―――080

MANILA ENCOUNTER

在馬尼拉的遭遇―――088

BRUSH OF MASTER MONK HSING YUN

星雲大師的毛筆―――102

A TRAVELING ORCHESTRA ON A BOAT

船上的管弦樂隊―――116

FUTURE OF POTTERY TRADITION IN MYANMAR

緬甸傳統陶藝的未來―――130

RETURN TO ANCESTRAL VILLAGE AT 96

在九十六歲回到祖先的村莊————————————140

TAI O VILLAGE, SHRIMP SAUCE CAPITAL OF THE WORLD

大澳村，世界蝦醬之都————————————154

IS ONE HUNDRED THE NEW EIGHTY

現在的一百歲其實是新八十歲？————————168

HANGING COFFINS OF THE PHILIPPINES

菲律賓的懸棺————————————————182

A ONCE-EVERY-TWELVE-YEARS PILGRIMAGE

12 年一次的朝聖————————————————200

A NINE-DAY CIRCUIT AROUND THE PLATEAU

環行高原九天的旅程————————————214

DISCOVERING PHILIPPINES CULTURAL

AND LITERARY TREASURES

發現菲律賓的文化與文學瑰寶————————236

HEAD HUNTER NO MORE

獵頭人不再！————————————————258

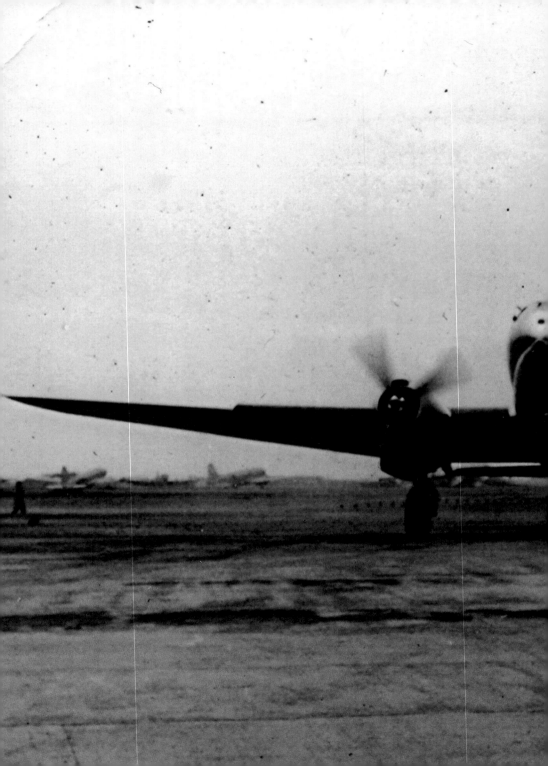

JACK YOUNG, A CENTENARIAN CHINESE PILOT AT 101

CX831 Inflight, New York to Hong Kong – June 13, 2015

JACK YOUNG，一百零一歲的中國飛行員

JACK YOUNG，一百零一歲的中國飛行員

「行啦！」*Jack Young* 有點不耐煩的說。「行啦！」，*Jack Young* 又說了一次。他的聲音很小但是口氣很堅定：「行啦」。

從他家走到兩條街口前的餐廳不用十分鐘，但 *Jack* 已經連著三次催促太太 *Louise* 走快點了。其實 *Louise* 每次停下來休息，也都是為了讓 *Jack* 在爬這段小坡時也能休息一下下，但是 *Jack* 每次都固執地拒絕。

他為什麼要停下來啊？到今年年底他就要一百零一歲了，他的堅持與毅力完全體現了「不斷向前」這個精神。每次見到 *Jack Young*，我都會跟他說，他應該把名字改成「*Jack Old*」，他覺得這提議還挺有意思的。

透過另一位出名的百歲飛行員陳文寬的介紹，我才有機會認識 *Jack Young*。*Jack* 在戰爭時飛越印度與中國的駝峰航線，剛開始時是陳文寬的副駕駛，後來成為中國航空公司（*CNAC*）的正機長。在那之前，約 *1930* 年的中期，他

JACK YOUNG,
A CENTENARIAN CHINESE PILOT AT 101

"Han la," urged Jack with a tone of impatience. That means "keep moving" in Cantonese. "Han la," there he went again. His voice was barely audible but firm. "Han la."

Within less than ten minutes, as Louise, his wife, walked Jack up the two blocks to get to the restaurant from their home, Jack repeatedly urged her along three times. Each time Louise stopped, trying to make Jack take a breather along the pavement with a slight grade, each time, Jack refused to stop.

Why should he stop? That insistence and perseverance had served him well, epitomizing his spirit of "keep moving" that had taken Jack from childhood to such a senior age, turning 101 later this year. Every time I saw Jack Young, I reminded him that he should tell people his name is "Jack Old". He seemed entertained whenever I mentioned it.

It was through Moon Chin, another centenarian and celebrity pilot; that I got

是廣州軍閥陳濟棠的空軍飛行員，之後才加入國民黨的空軍。如今 Jack 每個冬天都會為了避寒而離開加拿大的蒙特婁，因此我們第一次的見面是在香港。我訪問過他好幾次，不過這是第一次在他蒙特婁的家。

Jack（中文名楊積）1914 年 12 月出生於舊金山，父親來自澳門對面的廣東省中山縣。他的護照把出生年份登記成1917 年，這個美妙的錯誤讓他可以多工作幾年才退休，也讓他擁有更多時間與最愛的飛機相處。從飛行員退下後，他還是跟航空脫不了關係，他負責管理香港飛機工程公司的維修部門。這個維修部門的總部設在香港的啟德機場，這是他退休飛行後的職業……這，算什麼退休啊？

在 Jack 漫長的航空生涯裡有兩段最精彩的時期，第一段是 1930 年中期，經過二戰、中國內戰一直到 1950 年代前期。第二段是 1950 年的後期，那時共產黨已經掌控中國大陸了；這兩個時期是中國近代史上最動盪不安的日子，牽扯了不同的政黨，也牽扯到台灣與香港。

Jack 很坦白的說：「我從來都不覺得飛行很酷，但是我對它非常著迷。我也從不會誇說我是個飛行員。」「小時候，我一聽到飛機飛過來的聲音，我就會衝出屋外，不管是下課或是下班後，我都會去機場看飛機的起降……我一直都很清楚，有一天我一定也會在天上飛！」

to meet Jack. Jack started out as Moon's co-pilot, flying the Hump during the War between India and China until he was checked out as a Captain for the China National Aviation Corporation (CNAC). Before that, he flew for the Canton Warlord Chen Jitong in the mid-1930s, then joined the Kuomintang Nationalist Air Force. Our first meeting was in Hong Kong, where Jack spent each winter getting away from the bitter cold of Montreal. I had interviewed Jack several times. But this was the first time we met at his home in Montreal.

Jack was born in December 1914 in San Francisco. His father came from Zhongshan, a county adjacent to Macau in Guangdong Province of southern China. Jack's passport however, mistakenly bears his birth year as 1917, which allowed him to work a few more years before retiring. That was something he found most convenient, as it allowed him extra years around his beloved airplanes. By then, Jack was still involved with aviation, though not as a pilot, heading a team of maintenance personnel at the Hong Kong Aircraft Engineering Company (HAECO). The airplane servicing company had its home at Hong Kong Kai Tak Airport. This was the career Jack took up after "retiring" from active flying.

But the most exciting era of Jack's long career in aviation was during the early days, from the mid-1930s through World War Two and the Civil War years in China, continuing into the early 1950s when the Communists took over

Mainland China. Those were the most turbulent years of modern day China, involving various factions not only on the Mainland, but also in Taiwan and Hong Kong.

"I never thought that flying was a cool thing, I was just transfixed with flying. I never brag about it, trying to show-off by being a pilot," said Jack as a matter of fact. "As a kid, I used to rush out of the house whenever I heard an airplane flying overhead," he added. "After school and later after work, I always went over to the airfield to look at airplanes taking off and landing. I always knew somehow, some time, I would be up there flying.

"It was a promise I made to myself," Jack continued. "I worked hard, saving up every penny I had, so I could go to flight school. I even took up more than one job, I waited at tables, I did whatever job was on offer. I was only 16 at the time. But I said to myself. I will become a pilot. It was not cheap in those days to take flying lessons, as you know."

"You know, when I was a kid I used to wear glasses, and I had heard you must have good eyes to pass a flight test," recounted Jack. "Then one day I read in the Reader's Digest that looking at green fields and trees would help correct your eyesight," he recalled. "So I went out and looked intently at anything green, and over time it worked. Gradually I could do without my glasses," said Jack. It was such strong will that finally got Jack his flight license at age 19.

Jack's early flying career in US and Canton / Jack 早期曾在美國與廣東飛行

「這是我對自己的承諾，」Jack 繼續說：「我很努力工作，把每一毛可以省的錢都省下來，好讓我可以去上飛行學校。我甚至兼不只一份工，我當過餐廳的服務生，只要有工作機會我就去做，那時我才 16 歲，我跟自己說我要當一位飛行員。但是你也知道，那個年代要上飛行學校可是一點都不便宜。」

「你知道我小時候是戴眼鏡的，但是聽說飛行員一定要有好視力才能通過考試。」Jack 回憶著，「剛好有天我在讀者文摘上看到一篇文章說看綠色草原跟樹林會對視力有幫助，我就照做，出去盯著一切綠色的東西看，沒想到過了一陣子，還真的有用，漸漸的我視力回復到可以把眼鏡丟了！」Jack 堅決的意志讓他在 19 歲考上飛行執照，那年是 1933 年。

「在廣東時，我覺得我不只是在幫陳濟棠，我是為了中國而飛。我意識到當個中國人的重要，尤其在我經歷過被美國人歧視。」Jack 述說著他回到中國服務國家的原因。戰爭末期，他加入中國航空公司，一家中國政府與泛美航空合作成立的民航公司。

「駝峰是我飛行生涯最危險的一段。到處都是日本的戰鬥機，而且我飛的飛機都是沒有配備武器的民航機跟貨機。」Jack 回憶那個烽火戰爭年代。「為了要避開日本空

The year was 1933.

"In Canton, I felt I was flying for China, not just for Chen Jitong. I felt being Chinese is very important, and I could not stand being called Chinaman, Chink Chink, like that in America." Jack expressed his desire to go to China to serve the country. Later during the War, he joined CNAC, a civilian airlines and joint venture between the Chinese government and Pan American Airways.

"Flying the Hump was the most dangerous among my aviation career. The Japanese were everywhere with their Pursuit fighters, and we, flying passengers and cargo, were not armed," Jack recounted the most heady days of the War. "We had to fly high and into the cloud, mostly at night and bad weather, to avoid the Japanese while crossing the Hump," Jack added. "You just had to take full control of the plane, and be confident that you could do it. There was no second thought about danger or whatever." Jack held his fist firmly as he made his point. "I don't believe in luck. But I trust God, and thank him after each flight," Jack seemed to soften his tone when he mentioned his belief. "I went to church and prayed," he reminisced quietly.

By the 1950s, perhaps it was good measure that the airlines in Hong Kong chose not to let Jack get his hands behind the wheels inside a cockpit, but instead allowed him to maintain the aircrafts that he knew so well. Jack was

軍，我們得要飛得很高，深入雲層，而且大多是在夜晚或天候很差的時候。」「你只能全心全意的去掌握這架飛機，相信自己可以做得到。不允許自己有任何對危險的顧慮。」Jack 握緊拳頭的去強調。「我不相信運氣，但是我相信上帝，每趟飛行任務完成我都會感謝祂，」當他講到信仰時，頓時又柔和起來。「我會去教堂禱告」，他靜靜的回憶著。

到了 1950 年代，或許香港的航空界不欲 Jack 再重操機長之職，Jack 雖然不能再飛，但是他對航空業的專業足夠讓他去管理飛機的維修部門。Jack 不像其他的機師，一開始就當上機師，他的養成訓練是先當飛機維修師，然後才當上飛行員的。所以 Jack 對飛機的理解是從外到內的透徹。不過關於 Jack 的飛行紀錄，有一件事可能是個缺憾，也有可能是個好事，那要看你問的對象是誰。

大約 65 年前，當時 Jack 35 歲，他飛了一次最有爭議的航程。事件發生於 1949 年 11 月 9 號，毛澤東在天安門宣示中華人民共和國成立後約一個月。整晚無法入睡的 Jack，在外面還是一片漆黑時就起床，跟他一樣的，還有另外 11 個飛行員，以及 12 名副駕駛，跟無線電操作員。好像一個軍隊正在整隊，準備去執行重要的任務。

曙光乍現香港啟德機場，12 架飛機正在發動引擎，大部

after all trained first as a mechanic, before becoming a pilot. Unlike other pilots who went straight to the cockpit, he knew the aircraft well, inside and out. But there was one speck, of dirt or of merit, depending on who you speak to, on Jack's flying record.

This most controversial flight came about when Jack was a young man of 35, some 65 years ago. The episode happened on November 9, 1949, barely a month after Mao Zedong stood on Tien An Men Gate and proclaimed the founding of the People's Republic of China. On that particular morning, Jack woke up earlier than usual, before sunrise and when the sky was still dark without any sign of dawn, after a largely sleepless night. But he wasn't alone.

分是 *DC-3*、*C-47*（*DC-3* 的變種機型）、*C-46*，還包括一台才剛送到香港，最先進全新的 *Convair C-240*。引擎的轟鳴叫醒機場，這 12 架飛機，在 2 小時內陸續升空。座落在中國海岸的英屬殖民地上的機場官員，並未察覺有任何異常事情發生。畢竟這些飛機都是登記在兩家公司名下：中國航空公司和中央航空公司 (*Central Air Transport Corporation*，1945 年，戰後由陳文寬一起創辦的)。

在那時，大部分中國的西南方是由國民黨掌控著，像是桂林跟昆明。所以在國民黨的管轄內派出這兩家航空公司的飛機一點也不奇怪。但是當這些飛機升空後，他們卻修改了航道向東飛去，避開了國民黨的雷達跟無線電。接下來 5 個鐘頭，11 架飛機陸續降落在天津。其中最新的那架，屬於中央航空公司的，在北京著陸，這架飛機上載著 *CNAC* 及 *CATC* 這兩家公司的總經理，還有幾位共產黨的地下黨員，他們策畫這次行動已經好一段日子了。

兩座機場熱烈的歡迎這些飛機。事實上，到北京這架飛機上的工作人員跟旅客當天晚上都是周恩來晚宴的座上賓。毛主席也快速的為這些愛國飛行員寫下了讚美之詞。這確實是場政治事件，12 架飛機飛到剛成立的中華人民共和國；這也是中國民航航空的起點。飛行員在中國被視為起義英雄，被國民黨視為叛徒；然而，國民黨最後的處境是撤退到台灣這島嶼上。

There were eleven other pilots, and as many co-pilots plus radio operators wide awake on that early morning. It was as if a squadron was readying to go on some important war mission.

As the first shade of dawn gradually cast over Kai Tak Airport in Hong Kong, twelve airplanes, mostly DC-3, C-47 (a version of the DC-3), and C-46, including one most modern and a brand new Convair C-240 recently delivered to Hong Kong, all revved up their engines. The roar brought the airport to life, as one after another, these twelve airplanes took to the air in regulated succession within a period of two hours. The airport officials, controlled by the British in the tiny colony on the coast of China, did not suspect anything unusual. After all, these airplanes were registered with two civil aviation companies, CNAC and CATC (Central Air Transport Corporation, which was an airline co-founded by Moon Chin right after the end of the War in 1945).

At the time, much of southwest China was still in the hands of the Nationalists, including Guilin and Kunming. It wasn't unusual for the two airlines to dispatch their planes to cities under the jurisdiction of the Kuomintang. But as soon as these planes took to the air, they redirected their flight paths and veered far off to the east, avoiding radar and radio stations of the Nationalists. Within the next five hours, eleven of these planes would be landing in Tientsin in succession, and the newest plane, belonging to CATC, would touch down in Beijing. On that particular plane were the two General Managers of both

Captain Jack Young in 2016 / 機長 Jack Young，攝於 2016 年

CNAC and CATC, together with a few high-level underground communists who had choreographed the event over a long period of time.

There were great receptions at both airports. In fact, the Beijing crew and passengers were quickly whisked off to a welcoming banquet hosted by Zhou Enlai that same evening. Chairman Mao was soon to script some praising words for these brave and "patriotic" aviators. A coup indeed it was, when twelve airplanes defected to the newly founded PRC. This was to become the core of a fledgling young civilian airline for China. The defectors were hailed as heroes in China and as traitors by the Nationalists, who themselves had only retreated to the island of Taiwan not long before.

Jack Young was one of the pilots of the twelve airplanes, flying a C-46, which was considered a very new aircraft, developed and delivered only during the latter part of the Second World War. It was considered a very difficult airplane to fly, much larger and heavier than a DC-3. Many American flyers crashed and died in it. However, for Jack, this had always been his favorite airplane, powerful and spacious.

While most of the pilots who defected to China stayed, their fate through the 1950s and into the Cultural Revolution varied. No doubt the 50s were the glory days, but not for long, as the country became a nest of radicals who were finding every means to witch-hunt for anyone with any overseas connections.

Jack 是這 12 架飛機的其中一名機師，他飛的機型 *C-46*
當時是很新的，在二戰接近尾聲時開發出來的。這架比
DC-3 還難飛，因為它比較大也比較重。不少美國機師飛
這款飛機時都出事，人跟飛機都一起賠上。但是這款飛機
卻是 *Jack* 最喜歡的，因為有力又很寬敞。

大多數的機師都留在中國了，在 *1950* 年代到文化大革命
這段期間，每個人的命運都不同。*50* 年代確實是個燦爛
的年代，但過不久，這個國家變成一個激進派的溫床，極
盡所能的去尋找任何跟外國有關係的人，像在獵巫似的。
從國民黨過來的機師跟飛行人員自然成為獵物。

Jack 例外。他在中國飛了幾年，其中一段時間是當飛行教
練。*1952* 年他辭去在中國的工作，轉到香港，這也讓他
躲過了中國政治動盪不安的日子。縱使他是熱衷的民族主
義派，但是他從未效忠任何一個政黨。到今天，*Jack* 依
然覺得當一個中國人就應當要捍衛中國的尊嚴與完整，他
常常說「我們中國人不能丟臉」。但是，當他見識到政治
上的角力與運作已經擴及到航空業時，他又覺得他應該回
到香港。

那其實不是 *Jack* 的第一次反叛。在 *1930* 年中期，他是
軍閥陳濟棠旗下廣東空軍的機師，那時機師們集體帶著
飛機到南京投靠國民黨。*1949* 年發生的事，是他第二次

Pilots and crew who defected from the Nationalists to the Communists became natural prey.

Jack was one exception. He flew in China for only a couple of years, including time as a flight instructor. Then, in 1952, he decided this was not his cup of tea. He returned to Hong Kong and thus was spared the political turmoil of subsequent years in China. Though he was fiercely nationalistic, he did not pledge allegiance to any political party. Jack felt, even to this day, that as a Chinese he must uphold the dignity and integrity of China. An often repeated phrase from his mouth is, "We as Chinese cannot lose face." But early on, he saw the incessant political feuds and maneuvering within the government at all levels, including in the running of the airlines and its operations. He decided he should return to Hong Kong.

That incident was not Jack's first or only defection. In the mid-1930s, he was one of the pilots of the Canton Air Force under Warlord Chen Jitong. The pilots defected en masse with their airplanes to Nanjing to join the Kuomintang of the Nationalists. The 1949 debacle was his second round of defection.

Today, at such senior age, Jack still gets excited when talking about flying, especially when he displays his knowledge about each and every type of plane he has flown. But when asked about his defection to China, Jack will go "mum".

的叛變。

回到現在，一把年紀的 *Jack*，談到飛行時還是很興奮，尤其是當他告訴我每一款他所飛過的飛機時。但，當我問起從香港飛到中國的這件事情時，他卻沉默了。顯然，這是一件他不願回顧的事。我很清楚，*Jack* 親眼看過上個世紀中國的變化，而 *1949* 年，可能存在屬於他個人的遺憾與感傷，所以我沒有再追問下去。

與他們第一次的訪談是在石澳我們學會的 *1939* 航空展示廳，*Jack* 直挺挺地坐在我們模擬的 *DC-3* 機艙。第二次訪談，我刻意把機艙改成他最喜歡的機型 *C-46*。我們甚至把整面牆都貼上他早期飛行的照片，包括他還是學生時期在雙翼飛機裡的照片，還有他飛駝峰時的照片。他指向一張泛黃的照片說：「第一次看到飛機，我就知道我要當一位飛行員。」

他慢慢地敘述過往的事，且不時地重複著。我每次問他會不會擔心在那嚴峻的環境下飛行，他總是回答，「那是我的工作」。「我很了解這架飛機。而且我都會很仔細的檢查它，更何況我還是會修飛機的人。」

Jack 說：「你一定要真正的說服自己，你可以達到你的目標跟任務」，說這句話的時候他的聲音不大，但他舉起他

Obviously it is an episode he would much rather forget. Though I knew there was some personal loss resulting from that fateful decision in 1949, I did not want to bring it up in case that wound is still hurting him, a proud individual who had seen all the ups and downs of both China and Hong Kong throughout much of the last century.

At the first interview inside our aviation exhibit at the 1939 House in Shek O, Jack sat with his back straight in front of a life-size mock-up of a DC-3 cockpit. At our second interview, I surprised him by changing the cockpit to that of a C-46, his favorite airplane. We also had an entire panel decorated with early pictures of his flying career, including those taken when he was a student pilot in bi-planes, and pictures from the War years flying the Hump. He pointed to a picture, now turned yellow from age, of a young Jack Young. "Since seeing the first airplane, I knew I wanted to become a pilot."

He talked deliberately but slowly, often repeating his important points several times. Every time I asked whether he had been worried or afraid when flying under extreme conditions during the War, each time he would answer simply, "That was my job." "I knew my airplane and what it could do. I checked through the plane carefully, being trained also as a mechanic," Jack reiterated.

"You must be totally positive and fully convinced that you can achieve your goal and mission," said Jack with a firm but quiet voice while holding up his

的拳頭，以示堅定。穿著他的皮革飛行員夾克，脖子上還纏繞著絲巾，*Jack Young* 永遠都 *Young*，儘管他已經百歲了。

行啦，*Jack*！

fist to make his point. Immaculately dressed in his leather flight jacket with a tidy silk scarf around his neck, Jack Young will always remain young, even at over a hundred years of age.

Han la, Jack!

Jack in proud pose / Jack 的英姿

PILGRIMAGE LONG OVERDUE

姍姍來遲的朝聖

Zhongdian, Yunnan – July 10, 2015

姍姍來遲的朝聖

或許聽起來奇怪，我竟然是在達摩祖師洞去年被燒掉後才去朝聖的。達摩是第一位把佛教從印度帶到中國的祖師。這個洞穴離山腳約 1000 公尺，我從遠處看著它其實已經超過十年了。這裡就緊靠長江之西，我每年都會有好幾次的機會經過這個山腳，尤其是當我們從中甸中心出發到金絲猴／傈僳部落的路上時。

距離現在大約 400 年前，著名的明朝探險家徐霞客曾經靠著自己的雙腳與馬匹來到這山腳附近。當他抵達麗江時，政治上的因素迫使他回頭。不過那時候他的健康狀況也不好，未能到達目的地；他回到江蘇不久就過世了，那年他 55 歲。

直到一個月前，爬到山上寺廟的路仍是個 45 度的斜坡，得要花上 5 個鐘頭，對 65 歲的我來說並不是件容易的事。但是現在狀況不同了，也許是達摩祖師體恤像我這樣有些年紀的朝聖探險家，一條長 12 公里的水泥路剛剛鋪好，可以從山腳下開車盤繞著這座山直達寺廟，我還

PILGRIMAGE LONG OVERDUE

It seems strange that I should be making my first pilgrimage to Damuzong's meditation cave only after it was burnt down by fire last year. Damu was considered to be the First Patriarch Master who brought Buddhism from India to China. I've been looking up at this cave from far below, from some 1000 meters in elevation lower down at the foot of the mountain, for well over ten years. Every time, several times a year, we drove past the foot of this pinnacle peak rising west of the Yangtze River, on our way from our Zhongdian Center to the Golden Monkey/Lisu Hill Tribe site.

The renowned Ming Dynasty explorer Xu Xiake came this way on foot and horseback some 400 years ago. He came very close, arriving in Lijiang, but was turned back due to the political situation at the time. His ill health also prompted his return without achieving his goal, and he died soon after reaching home in Jiangsu at the age of 55.

Perhaps it was Damu's kind consideration for an aging pilgrim explorer like me. Up until a month ago, it would have taken me up to five hours to hike that huge gradient, with inclines of up to forty-five degrees, to reach the cave

真是幸運。

平常的日子這裡會有許多的朝聖者，但是今天下午我決定去這寺廟，路上沒有看到上下山的人或車子。在某些周末或是節慶會有很多人。在今天的中國，只有一個朝聖者去到這個這麼重要的佛教聖地確實是很少見的。也許是達摩祖師又再次給予這個朝聖者的賜福。

沿著這條路往上繞行，景色漸漸開闊，我的視線順著一水長江一路往下。長江曲折蜿蜒，時而隱身山後，時而現身，然後又消失在遠處的山谷裡。雲朵低懸在不遠天際，好像正在創作一幅中國的山水畫。

快到山頂的地方有些房子，其中一間是座很大的寺廟。達摩祖師洞藏在角落的懸崖邊。我對這些雄偉的房子沒什麼興趣，倒是去了一間老舊的小屋裡轉了一下經筒，然後就直接去這位智者的閉關洞穴。幾間殘破的建築物緊抓著懸崖，頓時鼓聲響起，好像在歡迎我們的到來。高高的階梯帶引我到一間佛堂，一位著藏紅袍的僧人正在點油燈。當地的藏族僧人扎西，指引我到這個神聖的地方，我奉獻了一點與這小寺廟規模相稱的香油錢。

沿著石階我走到一個超過百部經幡飄動的地方，傷痕累累的岩石被香火跟油燈燻的黑黑的。我用我的前額碰觸岩

Fertility rock by Damu Cave / 達摩祖師洞旁的求子石

temple, a trying endeavor for someone over 65 years of age. But recently, the situation has changed. A road, a cement-paved road, reaches the cave temple over a winding drive of 12 kilometers from the bottom. It was indeed a blessing for me.

On any usual day, there might be many pilgrims, but on today's afternoon when I decided to venture to the temple, no one, not a single car, was on the road up or down the mountain. It seemed a huge relief, as I have heard of the huge crowds on some weekends or special festive days. For China today, it is indeed rare to be a single pilgrim to an important Buddhist site. Perhaps Damu was again giving his blessings to this singular supplicant.

Qizhong Church / 茨中教堂

Up and up, as the road winded up, the scenery opened up. Down and down, as I looked down, my eyes followed the Yangtze further down. It curved and meandered, before disappearing behind a hill, only to reappear momentarily, before fading again into the distant hills. With low hanging clouds, a Chinese scroll painting was in the making.

Near the top, there was an ensemble of houses, including a huge temple. But Damu's cave was hidden around a corner precipice. I had no interest in grand buildings, but did turn a large prayer wheel inside a small old building, and went straight toward the meditation cave of the sage. A few more dilapidated buildings hugged the cliff face. The sound of drum momentarily started, as if welcoming my arrival. Tall steps brought me to a prayer chapel where a lone monk in saffron robe was attending to the oil lamps. I made a small offering in cash, commensurate with the small chapel. Tashi, a local Tibetan monk, pointed my way to the sacred site.

A short stairway with railings over the rocks brought me to where hundreds of prayer flags were fluttering. The rocks were scarred and darkened from incense and oil lamp offerings. I bowed and touched the rock with my forehead, later only to find out that this rock is where pilgrims come to make wishes for fertility. At 65, I hope my posturing would not be answered. The real cave was still a couple hundred meters around the cliff.

石，對祂行禮；後來我才知道，這岩石是朝聖者前來求子用的。今年我已經 65 歲了，希望我依樣畫葫蘆的祈禱千萬不會被實現。然而真正的達摩祖師洞距離懸崖還有二百公尺。

一座新的寺廟將會在今年完工，會有好幾層樓，傍著懸崖而建，這個重大的工程正在進行，但是天已經晚了，工人們都離開了。這個工程會在明年五月，最盛大的朝聖活動之前完工。猴年對達摩祖師洞來說是最重要的一年。在五月，第四個月亮升起的第一天，會有成千上萬的朝聖者

Snub-nosed monkey king / 金絲猴王

Major construction was going on though all workers had left, it being late in the day. A new multi-story temple would be finished by end of this year, hugging the cliff-face and enclosing the open cave. It would be done in time for the biggest pilgrimage next year in May. The Year of the Monkey in the twelve-year zodiac is the most important for Damuzong Cave. They are expecting tens of thousands would arrive, especially during the month of May, on the First Day of the Fourth Moon. For now, the cave was exposed and seemed cleared of all previous statues and offerings, having been burnt out. I bowed and folded my hands with a simple prayer, hoping that I could return next year for that special occasion.

On my way down the hill, I stopped at the Buddhist college affiliated to Damuzong Cave. Gongjiu, a lama at 48 years of age, was teaching a dozen or so young monks. We sat down for tea and chatted. He had been ordained thirty years ago as a teenager. A local Tibetan but with acute Han features, he had been here for decades. I was interested in his private abode overhanging the cliff, steps away below Damu's Cave. It had a courtyard overlooking the Yangtze below.

Could I stay there next May? He affirmed with a yes, and said it would be free. Free of charge only. As it may not be freed up in time by May. A solitary monk had been meditating inside for over three years, in one of the three rooms of the house. He would not want him disturbed. But if he

前來轉山；但是現在，被燒掉的洞穴裡空無一物。跟每個朝聖者會做的動作一樣，我對這個洞穴雙手合十，希望明年這特別的日子到來時，我也可以來參與。

下山時我們拜訪了跟達摩祖師洞有淵源的佛教學院。貢秋是一位 48 歲的僧侶，他在佛學院裡教書，學生大概有 12 位，都是年少的僧人。我們坐下來喝茶聊天，他說，他是 30 年前出家的，當時還只是個青少年。雖然貢秋是當地的藏人，但是他的五官卻跟漢人十分相像。我對他在懸崖上的住所很感興趣，因為離達摩祖師洞的下方只有幾步路而已，並且還有個小院子可以俯瞰山下的長江。

「明年五月我來的時候可以住這裡嗎？」我問。貢秋馬上回答可以，而且還不收費。但是前提是，房間得剛好有空。那個地方有三個房間，有個獨居的僧人在裡面已經閉關超過三年了，貢秋不希望外人去打擾他。依我的估計到了明年五月，這僧人應該已經出關了，我也應該可以住在這裡了。我祈禱這僧人在不久之後可以達到完全自由、寧靜、解脫的境界。

這趟旅途，我去了幾個不同信仰的聖地，除了達摩祖師洞之外，其他的地方我都很熟悉。當我在達摩祖師洞時，我們暑期的實習生正忙著視察金絲猴。每年我們辦的傈僳族弩弓節也都在這時候。然後是茨中的教堂，那是 19 世紀

should complete his meditation and exit by May, I would be most welcome to stay there. I prayed that the monk's next cycle closing on nirvana would be completed shortly.

On this trip, I was on a circuit pilgrimage to several sites of various religions, all familiar to me except Damuzong Cave. While I was visiting the Cave, our summer interns were busy observing the Snub-nosed Monkeys. Then the Lisu Crossbow Festival we organized yearly came and went. Next stop, the Church of Qizhong, founded by priests of the French Foreign Mission in the late 19th Century and later operated by the Grand St Bernard Mission of Switzerland between 1931 and 1951.

With my old friend Father Savioz's passing away almost two years ago in Martigny, I brought along my memories as I attended a solemn Friday Mass in the evening. It was interrupted by electric stoppage, but it was quickly resuscitated by a small generator. Father Yao Fei, a China-trained priest, was known to be hot tempered. But he treated me with grace, even allowing my team to film inside the church during service, whereas posters on the wall prohibited even photography.

As we drove for a long stretch along the Mekong, something delighted me. From what used to be a raw river spanned only by cable or rope bridges, today there are many suspension bridges, making crossing by locals far safer and

末由法國傳教士創立的，在 1931 年到 1951 年時，由瑞士耶次堡的聖伯納德教會持續運作。

兩年前我的老友沙智勇神父在瑞士瑪爾蒂尼結束了他在地球的一生；而我，則帶著對他的回憶前去參加週五晚上莊嚴的彌撒。彌撒中途突然停電，但是很快的，小台發電機的運作又讓彌撒繼續。姚飛神父，這位在中國學成的神父，大家都知道他的脾氣不是很好，但他卻賜予我恩典，讓我的團隊進去這個不允許攝影的教堂裡，拍攝了整個彌撒的過程。

沿著湄公河走，我發現一件讓我開心的事。從前那個用電纜和繩子連結的一座危橋，現在多出了幾個支撐，已經變成了一座安全的橋了，它不僅能讓當地人迅速安全的通過，連汽車跟拖拉機都不成問題。

不過有件事還是困擾著我。雄偉的湄公河竟然有好幾段被攔截，為了蓋水壩做水力發電，並且還有好幾座發電廠的工程仍在進行。沿著湄公河的村落只能無奈地接受這些水壩，這些水壩將生產的電輸送到大城市，甚至出口到鄰近的國家；然而這附近村民到現在還是常常會遇到斷電的問題，就像今天的彌撒，會有這樣的情況，其中肯定出了很大的問題。

efficient. Many can even be crossed by cars or tractors.

But something else also bothered me. It seemed strange and illogical that several dams now cut across the mighty Mekong, providing electricity in abundance through hydro plants. Others are in process of being finished. Villages along the Mekong play host to these series of dams, with electricity generated and channeled into the power grid that supports entire big cities or is even exported to neighboring countries. Yet villagers have had to put up with electric shortage and outage regularly, every night, for ages, until even today. Something is gravely wrong.

An hour or so past Qizhong is CERS' former clinic/teahouse. It was completed in 2003 to serve pilgrims during the special Year of the Sheep, when tens of thousands of Tibetans arrived from all over the plateau to circumambulate sacred Khawakarpo Mountain. During six months within that summer, our clinic served over 4,600 patients, and we offered thousands more cups of buttered tea. This year again is the Year of the Sheep, and pilgrims would arrive again in droves. But twelve years on, the teahouse is in a ruined state, having been taken over by the local villagers who did not care to maintain it; a case of poor custodianship.

I stopped for two nights at our former Tibetan Mastiff Kennel site. Guji is a pristine village with only five families, three of which are still practicing

Primrose at lake about cheese site / 氂牛乳酪工廠湖邊的報春花

polyandry, looking directly at the spectacular Khawakarpo range. I had not stayed here for over five years, though I had passed through several times en route to or from Tibet. As if to welcome my return, Khawakarpo decided to show his face, a rarity during the summer rainy season. It is usually veiled in fog and clouds.

The Mastiff project had been suspended for several years due to the astronomical prices paid by speculators for such great canines. We felt a continued effort would be ineffective, as puppies handed out to Tibetans would be turned around and sold in the market. More recently, that fad had fizzled, and there were reports that breeders had even sold their now worthless mastiffs to butchers.

Today, our beautiful site with several well-situated lodges had just found a new custodian. Wang Mei, a successful entrepreneur turned devoted Buddhist, intends to turn it into an

經過茨中約一個小時就是 CERS 之前的項目點，診所和茶屋。那是 2003 年蓋好的，一個特別的羊年，成千上萬來自高原各地的藏人都來到這個神聖的卡瓦卡博轉山。這診所和茶室就是用來服務這些朝聖者的。六個月之間我們的診所照顧了超過 4,600 個病人，奉上的酥油茶有數千上萬杯。今年又是羊年，肯定又會有大批的朝聖者前來。不過十二年過去了，這地方也已經毀了，接管的當地村民並沒有好好的維護這個地方；神山腳下的診所和茶室，不幸地成為管理者失職的個案。

我在之前藏獒項目的大本營「古久」停留了兩晚。古久是個天然未受汙染的村莊，直接面對著卡瓦卡博神山，村裡只有五戶人家，其中三戶採一妻多夫制。我已經有五年沒有在這停留，但是每次往來西藏都會經過這裡。這次卡瓦卡博決定露出祂的臉，好像是在歡迎我的到來，這景象在夏天的雨季是很少見的，通常山頭都會被厚厚的雲霧罩住。

藏獒犬的復育計畫已經停擺了好幾年，因為投機者的介入把藏獒的價錢炒到一個天價。我們覺得如果把藏獒的幼犬送給藏人們，最終的命運也只是會被賣出去而已。而最近，藏獒的這股熱潮似乎開始退去，還有報導說，有些不肖的繁殖者甚至把不值錢的藏獒犬賣給了屠夫。

我們這個美麗的地方有幾間位置很好的民宿，並且有了一

eco-lodge catering to Buddhist pilgrims, monks on meditation retreat, and a stopover for NGO's keen on nature and culture conservation. We hope this would give this wonderful site a new lease on life.

My next stop was Dongjulin Nunnery. Here the CERS project was started in 1999 and lasted several years. Over that period, four dormitories were constructed for the nuns before another team could move in to restore the Assembly Hall, roof and all. Finally the ten walls of ancient murals were painstakingly cleaned and stabilized. Along the way, two books and one documentary film were made. At the time there was no road up the mountain and we had to hike for almost an hour to reach the nunnery.

Today a fully paved road ends at a monumental gate as entrance into the nunnery. Many new buildings, big and decorative, had been built, thanks to more substantial funding from the government and newly successful Tibetan and Chinese supplicants. I feel gratified that, at the time of dire need, CERS was here to support and facilitate conservation efforts.

The nuns were totally surprised to see me showing up. After all, it had been years since my last visit. I could tell their joy was genuine, as they poured me bowl after bowl of buttered tea. Through a doctor-nun who spoke Chinese, the head nun told me that "I", meaning my team, was like their parents giving them a rebirth. I felt very moved that they should remember those hardship

個新的經營管理者。王梅是個成功的企業家，也是一位虔誠的佛教徒，她計畫把這裡的房子變成生態旅館，服務來朝聖的佛教徒與禪修的出家人。這是一個對自然與文化保育有熱情的創意。我們希望王梅能為這個很棒的地方開創出全新的生命。

我的下一站是東竹林尼姑寺。一九九九年 CERS 開始在這裡進行項目，並持續了好幾年。那段時間，先蓋了四間宿舍給尼姑，之後另一組團隊進入大殿修復壁畫。最後終於修復及保存了那十片牆面上的古老壁畫。這一路上，出版了兩本書也做了一個紀錄片。回想當時還沒有車路可以到山上，我們要徒步快一個鐘頭的山路才到得了尼姑寺。

現在有一條鋪好的路直通尼姑寺壯觀的大門。寺裡也蓋了很多新的建築，很大而且裝飾的很好，這都得感謝政府給予的資金還有西藏的新富豪與中國的贊助者。我感到欣慰，在尼姑寺最需要的時候，CERS 曾經在這裡支持跟協助這項文化保護工作。

尼姑們看到我非常驚訝。因為我上一次來這裡已經是多年前的事了。當她們為我倒上酥油茶的時候，我可以看的出來她們發自內心的真誠喜悅。透過會說普通話的藏醫尼姑翻譯，老尼姑告訴我，「我」（意思是我們團隊）就像她們的再生父母。我很感動她們還記得那段艱苦的日子。巴

days. Balaganzong, the sacred mountain facing the nunnery, seemed to concur. It gracefully revealed its pyramid peak as our parting gift.

As my last stop on this journey, I took another detour and went to visit our Yak Cheese Factory. It seemed necessary to deliver in person the great news that we had received just two weeks ago. A customer in Beijing, without our knowing, had entered our yak cheese at the annual cheese contest in France. We were nicely surprised that our cheese took a Gold Award, not an easy feat in the culinary capital of the world. The blooming wild flowers in the high country seemed to join in celebrating this good news, making this moment even sweeter with fragrance.

As a finale to this pilgrimage, both to sacred sage cave and mountains, as well as to our many project sites, I decided to bring our most beloved mastiff back to our Zhongdian Center. Chili is now eleven years old, two years past the average age that Tibetan Mastiff are known to live. He had been retiring at our yak cheese site with his life-long partner Ah Yee. But Ah Yee passed away about six months ago, and Chili was left alone in his yard. I wanted Chili to live out his life with dignity. He joined CERS as a four-month old puppy at our Zhongdian Center, in 2004.

After all, he had been on a full page of the Wall Street Journal, and joined me on a front page story of that prestigious newspaper. He was on the face of a

拉更宗是面對尼姑寺的神山，似乎也有同感。祂優雅地露出山峰就像是給我們道別的禮物。

這趟旅程的最後一站，我特地繞到我們的氂牛乳酪工廠。親自去告訴他們我兩周前收到的消息才比較恰當。一位在北京的客戶，在未告知我們的情況下把我們的氂牛乳酪拿去參加每年在法國舉辦的乳酪競賽。令人驚喜地，我們的乳酪拿下金獎，在世界美食首都拿到這獎項確實是不容易。高原上盛開的野花似乎也在慶祝這個好消息，讓此刻的甜蜜更添加了些芬芳。

從達摩祖師洞到神山，還有我們許多項目點之後，我決定將摯愛的藏獒帶回中甸中心，作為這趟朝聖的壓軸。Chili 現在已經十一歲了，比一般藏獒的平均壽命還多了兩年，牠退休後跟一輩子的夥伴 Ah Yee 住在我們的氂牛乳酪工廠。但是六個月前 Ah Yee 過世了，Chili 孤零零的在牠的院子裡。我希望 Chili 有尊嚴的過完牠的一生。二零零四年 Chili 四個月大的時候加入 CERS 的中甸中心。

牠上過華爾街日報的整頁報導，跟我一起在這個聲望很高的報紙上過頭條。牠也曾出現在中國的郵票，也跟主播 Richard Quest 上過 CNN。為我們旗艦藏獒安置一個最終的家，讓牠有個美好的結局，或許正反應了我希望在晚年也有個適合我的家。

Chinese stamp. He appeared on CNN with anchor Richard Quest. Perhaps giving Chili, our flagship mastiff emeritus, a final home with happy ending may reflect on how I wish to find a worthy home for myself at old age.

Happy nuns / 開心的尼姑們

Mr. Wu Tianfu accompany Chairman Mao meeting dignitaries /
吳田夫陪同毛主席接見外交使節

回憶七十年前的歷史

REMEMBERING HISTORY, SEVENTY YEARS AGO

Katha, Myanmar – August 15, 2015

回憶七十年前的歷史

1945 年 8 月 15 日。那時我還沒有出生，是在我出生前的四年。但回憶可以透過我父親和他的友人持續存在。1941 年太平洋戰爭開打，我父親在香港大學的醫學院讀到三年級，今年他 96 歲，當時是一個醫學院的學生，他跟同學們很快的被徵調到英國「志願」救護隊服務。

1941 年的聖誕節，不到兩週香港就失守了。英軍投降，父親不得不找個地方躲起來。香港被占領時，要繼續讀書接受教育的機會是很渺茫的。父親的教授是耶穌會教士，他傳來消息說，如果父親能和其他學生能一起到桂林，那麼他們就還有機會繼續念書。

即使來自富裕的家庭（我的祖父是捷成洋行的買辦），在那時若要離開香港，必需夜裡摸黑搭船到珠三角，然後再徒步到廣西省的桂林。況且在戰時的中國根本不可能讓他接受醫學教育，最後我父親選了一門跟醫學較接近的科目「化學」。戰爭結束前，他畢了業成為一個化學家。父親一生都在香港頂尖的學校裡教化學。

REMEMBERING HISTORY, SEVENTY YEARS AGO

August 15, 1945. Of course I wasn't even born, some four years short. But the memory is there, through my father and my friends. When War broke out in the Pacific in 1941, my father, now 96, was into his third year in Medical School at Hong Kong University. Being a student in medicine, as with his fellow classmates, he was quickly inducted into the "volunteer" ambulance services of the defending British.

Hong Kong was to fall within two weeks, on Christmas Day of 1941. With the surrender of the British forces, my father went into hiding. There was little hope of renewed education in a Hong Kong under occupation. Word came shortly thereafter from his professor, a Jesuit priest (my father stayed at Ricci Hall), that if he and fellow students could make it to Guilin, they would have a chance to continue with their studies.

Despite being from a well-to-do family, my grandfather being comprador of the Jebsen Company, my father had to leave Hong Kong in the dark of night in a boat to the Pearl River Delta, and walked his way to Guilin in Guangxi

Province. No more medical education was possible in war time China, so my father pursued the closest discipline; Chemistry. He would graduate before the war ended, as a chemist. That led to a life-time career teaching science at one of the leading schools of Hong Kong.

My mother came to Hong Kong as a teenager, from a well-to-do Swatow trading family. She met my father before the war, and they made vows to marry, but were separated during the entire remaining years of the War. Marriage did not materialize until the War ended, almost four years later. The Japanese surrendered on August 15, 1945, seventy years to this day. Waiting out one's lover for years seemed quite normal in those days. Time was slow, life was more meaningful.

The War the Japanese waged disrupted a lot of lives. My parents were the lucky ones, not being killed, and even able to reconnect. Others had it worse; much worse. Dead people, however, cannot rise to tell their stories. So I will relate some from those who survived, as well as from those who are still living.

Wu Tianfu was an old friend who was my liaison officer, assigned by the Chinese government during my National Geographic years when I roamed remote China. Familiar to complex logistics and special requests, he had coordinated visits by Ho Chi-minh and even Che Guevara when they visited China. Wu was born in Swatow the same year as my father, 1919, to a

My father Mr Wong Chin Wah as a young boy scout / 作者父親黃展華年輕時童軍英姿

我母親十幾歲的時候來到香港，家裡也算富裕，在汕頭做貿易。她跟父親在戰前相識後誓言結為連理，但是戰爭讓他們分隔兩地。將近四年後直到戰爭結束，他們才結婚。70 年前的 1945 年 8 月 15 日，日本投降。在那個年代花上幾年的時間去等候你愛的人似乎是很正常的，時間在那時走得很慢，但是生命卻更有意義。

日本挑起的戰爭破壞了所有人的生活與生命。我父母很幸運，沒在戰爭中丟了命，而且戰後還可以重逢。但是有很多人的境遇就沒這麼好了，而且可以說是很慘的，非常非常慘。死掉的人沒法起身訴說他們的故事，所以我會試圖從生存下來的人，還有些現在還在的人的身上，轉述他們的故事。

吳田夫是我的「老」朋友，那時我還在美國〈國家地理雜誌〉遊走中國偏遠地區時，他是中國政府派給我的聯絡窗口。他接待過胡志明甚至切‧格瓦拉，他對後勤和特殊要求一點也不陌生。田夫 1919 年出生在汕頭，跟我父親同年，家族從事貿易，很富有，他出生後不久就前往到新加坡。1937 年日本侵略中國，那年田夫還在讀高中。

其實，早在西方世界知道以及開始同情中國的處境時，日本就已經開始侵略中國了，時間可以推到 1895 年，這年中國把台灣割讓給日本。接著在 1931 年日本侵略滿州，

wealthy trading family, but soon left for Singapore. Wu was studying in high school when Japan invaded China in 1937.

In real terms, the Japanese invasion started in 1895, long before western knowledge or sympathy sided with the Chinese. That year, China lost Taiwan to the Japanese. Then in 1931, they invaded Manchuria, but Chiang Kai-shek was helpless and kept quiet regarding that invasion, since the region was under the control of Chinese warlords, not the Kuomintang party that he led. But with the escalation of aggression in July 7, 1937 as the Japanese army entered Beijing, Chiang finally declared war on Japan.

Reading in newspapers and hearing by radio about the danger China faced, Wu Tianfu, being a patriotic overseas Chinese, went on the streets and joined demonstrations against the Japanese invaders. The British dispersed the protests and Wu's father sent him off to Vietnam so that he could focus on learning about business. Instead, with a friend in Saigon, Wu left for Chongqing and, through General Ye Jianying, managed to arrive in Yenan where he joined the Red Army. The year was 1939. Wu was barely 20 years old.

Throughout the War, Wu stayed with the Communists, living among the loess hill caves of Yenan. During the following ten years, Wu Tianfu kept a stamp collection. I know others who collect stamps, but no one else who

蔣介石也很無助，因為這裡受當地軍閥控制，並不是他的國民黨可以有影響力的地方，所以他選擇沉默。但是當日本進一步侵略到北京時，蔣介石終於向日本宣戰，那是 1937 年 7 月 7 日。

從報紙、廣播得知中國的處境後，在新加坡的吳田夫，這位愛國華僑跟著群眾一起上街抗議日本的侵略，英國人驅散了這些抗議的群眾。然後，田夫的父親把他送去越南，希望他可以繼續學做生意。人沒留在越南，他卻跟一位西貢的朋友前往重慶，透過葉劍英的安排，到了延安從參軍。那是 1939 年，田夫還不到 20 歲。

整場戰役，田夫一直跟著共產黨住在延安的黃土洞裡。在那十年裡，田夫收集郵票。我知道有人收集郵票，但是不知道有人只收藏一組郵票。六張一套，總共超過六百張。田夫在延安收的這些郵票，全是在共產黨全面掌控中國前發行的，上面印有著名的唐朝延安寶塔。這些郵票也曾刊登在幾本郵票目錄的封面，專題是解放前的共產黨郵票。

1945 年 8 月 15 日，日本投降的那一天，一聽到消息，田夫馬上就衝到延安的郵局，把好幾張郵票蓋上日期。這日期章對田夫來說有重大的意義，這是充滿喜悅的一天，特別的回憶。不是因為在 1945 年田夫預測這些少見的郵票

collects stamps and keeps only one kind of stamp. Six to a set, with a total of over 600 stamps. Wu Tianfu's stamps of Yenan, from a time before the Communists came to power in China, have the famous Tang dynasty pagoda on it. This stamp also graces the cover of several stamp catalogues featuring pre-liberation Communist stamps of China.

On the day the Japanese surrendered, Aug 15, 1945, Wu, upon hearing the news, rushed to the post office in Yenan, and had several of his stamps chopped. That chop added immense value to Wu, as a special memory of that joyous day. Not because, in 1945, Wu could predict the speculated prices of rare stamps that would escalate in the coming decades, or because he knew ahead that the Communists would take over the entire Mainland some four years later. It was simply to remember the hard-won War.

Besides, had Wu Tianfu been interested in the monetary value of such a stamp set, he would not have had his widow pass them down, all 600 some stamps, to me after his death. Wu passed away ten years ago in Guangzhou. He never returned to Singapore after the War, except once when he was very advanced in age, and only to visit his relatives. The War had separated a bright and passionate young man from his parents, forever.

Three of my most senior friends were all born in 1914. Moon Chin in April, Peter Goutiere in September and Jack Young in December, now living

在未來的幾十年會變得很值錢，或是四年後共產黨會全面接掌中國；而是這些郵票記憶的是一個得來不易的勝利。

況且如果田夫是對這些郵票的價錢這麼在意的話，他就不會讓他的夫人在他過世之後請夫人把六百多張的郵票交到我的手上。十年前田夫在廣州過世，在此之前，他從未回到新加坡居住，只有在他晚年的時候回去過一次，當時是為了拜訪親戚。這場戰爭，讓一位聰明有熱情的青年與他的父母永遠分隔。

我的長輩友人裡有三位都是出生在 1914 年。陳文寬生在四月，*Peter Goutiere* 是九月，*Jack Young* 則是十二月。他們現在分別住在舊金山，紐約跟蒙特婁。今年五月我到美國加拿大時，一一拜訪過這三位老人家。

in San Francisco, New York and Montreal respectively. I visited all three centenarians earlier this year in May when I was in the U.S. and Canada.

While they are 101 this year, 70 years ago, as young men, they were all pilots, flying war supplies and passengers across the infamous Hump over the Himalayas from India to China. Sea routes were not feasible, as the enemy controlled all sea lanes and ports along the coast. This dangerous air route became the lifeline for a distressed China under attack by the Japanese.

Over a thousand pilots and hundreds of planes were lost flying the Hump. Moon, Peter and Jack were not just the lucky ones, but the most experienced and capable among pilots flying for CNAC. Peter was among the pilots who flew the most missions across the Hump, a total of over 700 flights. All three pilots lost dear friends during the War. Moon lost much of his own belongings as he was evacuating officers and common people from cities like Shanghai, Guangzhou and Hong Kong. Such experience altered the lives and destinies of all young men who became involved in the War.

Moon also captained the C-53 that brought General Doolittle out of China after the Tokyo Raid, when Doolittle's squadron took off from an aircraft carrier and bombed Japan's capital. On that same flight from Kunming to India, Moon stopped to evacuate 70 refugees out of Myitkyina, just as the

Moon Chin Chen, Jack Young, Peter Goutiere (from left to right) /
陳文寬・楊積・Peter Goutiere（左到右）

今年他們全都一百零一歲了！七十年前他們都是年輕的飛機師，載著戰爭時的補給品和旅客，從印度飛到中國，飛過那著名的駝峰，越過喜馬拉雅山。海線在當時是不可行的，因為沿岸的路線跟港口都被敵軍控制住。在日本的攻擊下，這條危險的空中航線可是戰火中維繫中國的命脈。

超過一千位的飛行員跟好幾百架的飛機在飛駝峰時失事。陳文寬、Peter 跟 Jack 不只是非常的幸運，他們也是中國航空公司 (CNAC) 經驗最老道，能力最強的飛行員。為了執行任務，Peter 飛駝峰超過七百趟。這三位機師都在戰爭裡失去過摯友。陳文寬曾經從上海、廣州、香港等大城市裡將軍人和平民撤出時，陳文寬失去他大部份的財產。參與這場戰役的年輕人，他們的生命與命運全都改變了。

杜立德將軍的縱隊去轟炸日本的首都之後，陳文寬駕駛 C-53 負責將他載離中國。這趟從昆明到印度的飛行，發生在日本人快逼近機場的時候。陳文寬繞去密支那接走 70 位難民，但是，C-53 是 DC-3 的改版，最多只能載 28 位乘客。就在準備起飛的時候，坐在活動座位的杜立德將軍問文寬「你清楚你在做什麼事嗎？」陳文寬回憶著他當時的回答：「難民一點也不重」。這件事創下了 C-53 機型的一項紀錄。

戰爭在這些飛行員、亞洲人以及全世界上的人心中，留下

Japanese were closing in on the airport and surrounding it. The C-53, a version of the DC-3, usually maxed at 28 passengers. As they prepared to take off, Doolittle, sitting in the jump seat, asked Moon, "Do you know what you are doing?" Moon recalls he answered, "Refugees don't weigh very much." That remains a record for such an air plane.

The War years left an indelible mark on all these pilots, as it did on so many people in Asia and throughout the world.

As I am writing this, I am sailing on the Irrawaddy, from Katha toward Mandalay. This entire region, remote as it is, was devastated and overrun by the Japanese. The Irrawaddy Flotilla Company, then the largest freshwater fleet in the world, had to scuttle almost all of its 600 some ships to prevent them from falling into Japanese hands.

On the Japanese side, of over 350,000 Japanese soldiers deployed to Burma between 1942 and 1945, 180,000 of them died. Many didn't even know clearly what they died for, except that the order was out to fight and kill, issued by the war monger generals of the Imperial Japanese Army. In an account written by Kazuo Tamayama, he recounted the miseries of the common Japanese soldier in Burma. It was both moving and shocking, as it described the last days of the Japanese stand inside the jungle.

了不可磨滅的印記。

寫這篇文章的時候我正航行在伊洛瓦底江，從卡塔出發，目的地曼德勒。這個偏遠的地區曾經被日本人蹂躪，滿目瘡痍。在那時候，伊洛瓦底船公司，擁有世界上最大的淡水船隊，為了避免船隻落到日本人的手裡，船公司緊急破壞了將近 600 艘的船，幾乎是他們全部的船。

而在日本這一方，1942 年到 1945 年間超過 350,000 位日本軍人被派到緬甸，其中有 180,000 位喪命。許多喪失生命的人並不知道他們失去生命是為了什麼，他們只是接受日本皇軍嗜血好戰將領們的指令，命令他們去打殺。*Kazuo Tamayama* 的回憶錄裡記載一般日本軍在緬甸慘痛的故事。戰爭接近尾聲時日本人在叢林裡發生的事，觸目驚心，有些也動人心弦。

幾年前我曾聽說過，有年輕的日本人來到密支那北部的墓園去為當時因為戰爭而喪命的人致意。他們很低調，或許是因為羞愧。我希望他們的羞愧並不是因為戰敗，而是悔過他們曾經帶給這麼多的人也包括他們自己巨大的痛苦與苦難。

如果人類從戰爭中沒有學到任何教訓，歷史將會再重演。

Several years ago in Myitkyina further to the north, I heard accounts about young Japanese visiting the cemetery to pay homage to their war dead. They did so quietly, perhaps because of shame. I hope it was not in shame of losing the War, but remorse in bringing so much pain and suffering to so many people and countries around Asia, including their own.

If the lesson of war of aggression is not learned, history will surely repeat itself.

Wu Tianfu's stamps of Yenan, dated on the day the Japanese surrendered, Aug 15, 1945 / 吳田夫收藏 1945 年 8 月 15 日抗戰勝利時延安郵票

喬治・歐威爾在緬甸日子下的影子

SHADOW OF GEORGE ORWELL'S BURMESE DAYS

Katha, Myanmar – August 15, 2015

喬治・歐威爾在緬甸日子下的影子

這殖民地時代蓋的房子直到現在還保留著那時的一絲繁華。深紅色的磚，柚木橫欄，角落的柱子，偌大的正門鑲著片片玻璃，這些都一一訴說著那個年代的故事，那個英國軍官威風凜凜地進駐這棟樓房的年代。

這裡應該會有一個管家，或許幾位女傭和侍從，一、二個園丁，肯定還有位馬車車夫！這是喬治・歐威爾筆下的緬甸，當時他是一位警官，住在伊洛瓦底江西岸的卡塔。離這棟房子不遠處有個俱樂部，緊鄰著網球場，直到一年前，大家都以為這棟紅、棕相間的房子就是喬治・歐威爾曾經住的，所以都稱這棟為喬治・歐威爾的家。

不過 Phyo Ko 並不這麼認為，他是個業餘的歷史學家，也是個喬治・歐威爾迷。2014 年，在 Phyo Ko 的一番考究下，他認為這棟紅棕相間的房子是歐威爾在《緬甸歲月》書中，那位虛構人物麥克格瑞格先生所居住的房子。他並且認為歐威爾真正住過的房子是離這棟幾條街外的一棟半殖民式，並以柚木蓋的建築物。那棟建築物的屋

Downstairs porch / Entrance to hous ・ 樓下走廊 / 入口大門

SHADOW OF GEORGE ORWELL'S BURMESE DAYS

The colonial house still retains a shade of its former glory. Bricks in crimson red, teak wood cross-bars and corner pillars, a large front door with glass panels tell tales of an era past, when British officers would take up the residence with pomp and circumstance.

A butler there would be, and perhaps several maids and attendants, a gardener or two, certainly a carriage driver; those were the days George Orwell described, when he lived in Katha, on the west bank of the Irrawaddy River, as a police officer. Not far down the road from the house was the Club House, nearby to a tennis court. Up until a year ago, everyone thought this red and brown house was where George Orwell stayed, and it was known

House Orwell described / 歐威爾筆下的緬甸房子

簷、陽臺、階梯都有非常緬甸風格的裝飾。不管怎麼樣，這兩棟都是很重要的歷史建築物，因為它們述說著歐威爾怎麼從一個英國伊頓貴族中學的公子到後來成為民主社會主義的信奉者。

為了審慎起見，這兩棟房子我都去參觀了，也算是我的朝聖之旅，這位名作家所寫的《動物莊園》、《1984》都是我中學時必讀的書。喬治・歐威爾應該是一位連緬甸政府也認為值得緬懷和表揚的一個人。畢竟在他的寫作裡，

simply as George Orwell's house.

But Phyo Ko, a Burmese Orwell fanatic and amateur historian, thought otherwise. Phyo Ko, after some exhaustive research, claimed in 2014 that this house should be the one Orwell described in his book Burmese Days, taken up by the fictional Mr. MacGregor, a colonial officer. Phyo Ko believed Orwell lived a few blocks away, in another semi-colonial house, a teak house with some Burmese motifs on the eaves, on the verandahs and on the stairs. Both houses, however, are important as relics to illustrate Orwell's significant transition, from an Etonian to a democratic socialist.

To be on the safe side, I visited both houses, as I am on sort of a pilgrimage to old haunts of this famous English writer, the man who authored Animal Farm and 1984, both must-reads during my college days. George Orwell is someone the Burmese government should feel safe to remember and honor. After all, his writing demeaned the British colonial system and its policies, and the opulence and decadent lifestyle of the colonialists; all in line with current official sentiments about that era.

It seems strange that someone as conscious as Orwell was about the ills of colonialism, defying the system that he worked for, would also write such critical satire about totalitarian states and society throughout his later writings. But Animal Farm is a classic allegory portraying the defects and

他貶低英國的殖民制度與政策，並批判殖民者在那過著奢華的生活；回頭看這段歷史，他的描述、觀察跟今天官方的看法是一致的。

說來奇怪，像歐威爾這樣有意識的人，居然會對殖民主義這樣反感，他根本就在對抗他所屬的群體和體制；他晚年在作品裡狠狠的嘲諷極權主義下的國家與社會。《動物莊園》裡經典的寓言描述共產主義與法西斯主義的缺陷，還有難以避免的貪腐。

喬治‧歐威爾在緬甸快五年的時間裡，在卡塔待了一年，從 1926 年到 1927 年。他在卡塔的日子為他在 1934 年出版的第一本小說《緬甸歲月》打下很好的底子。他的寫作所帶來的影響之大，以至於他的名字也成為了個形容詞 ──「歐威爾主義」，代表極權政府下的社會是沒有是非的，連謊言都可以被當成真相。這讓我想到世界上另外只有一個人，他的名字同時也是人家常用的形容詞，柏拉圖。

現在，喬治‧歐威爾所描述的房子已經成了廢墟。你可以從側門走進去欣賞這棟兩層樓的殖民年代的建築物，裡面有四個壁爐，每層樓各有兩個。木製的階梯連接樓層，從百葉窗看出去的是大樹，大樹後面襯著是一片田野。

House Orwell lived / 歐威爾曾住過的房子

我靜靜的站在客廳的壁爐邊，謹慎地環視四周。一刻，我彷彿可以聽到來自一世紀前的腳步聲，從樓梯那端傳來。我看到一個人影映照在一道門的玻璃上。「喬治」，我心想。頓時，我發現那是我自己的倒影。但那短暫的一刻，我還真的以為我見到喬治‧歐威爾本人呢。

Shadow of George Orwell / 喬治‧歐威爾的影子

inevitable corruption, not only of communism, but of fascism as well.

George Orwell stayed in Katha, only for a year from 1926 to 1927, during the last part of his almost five years in Burma. His experience at Katha formed the basis of his first novel, Burmese Days, published in 1934. His writings were to affect a generation of readers, resulting in his name becoming even an adjective; "Orwellian" became a reference and synonym for a totalitarian government and society that passes off lies as the truth. I can only think of one other name of a person becoming a commonly used adjective, Plato.

Today, the house George Orwell described is abandoned. One can enter through a side door and appreciate the emptiness of a two-story colonial house, with four fireplaces, two to each floor. A wooden stairs leads up to the upper floor where I could look out louvre windows into big trees and the field beyond.

I stand quietly by the fireplace chimney in the living room and look around discretely. For a moment I feel as if I can hear footsteps from almost a century ago, coming down the stairs. I see a shadow, reflected off the glass panes of a partition door. "George, I presume," I think of asking. Suddenly, I realize it is just a reflection of myself. But for a short moment, I thought I was meeting George Orwell in person.

蓮花絲巾，在 *Nang* 的家中

LOTUS SCARF

Inle Lake, Myanmar – August 20, 2015

蓮花絲巾，在 *Nang* 的家中

釋迦牟尼佛最經典的姿勢是坐在蓮花上冥想。傳說祂身上穿的袍是用蓮花莖抽絲織布而成的。因此在東方，蓮花往往跟純淨，平靜，尊敬連結在一起。

在撣邦的茵萊湖，緬甸的北邊，這種古老的傳統織布方式到現今還保存著。*Nang* 是這間創於 *1932* 年工作坊的第三代傳人，從最初十牀織機到今天過百台。繰絲及織造還是他們主要的工作，蓮花絲巾是他們最寶貴也最引以為傲的產品。

直到今天，遠從日本來的和尚、眼光挑剔的法國、德國、

LOTUS SCARF

From the House of Nang

The Buddha Gautama is often featured in an iconic position, seated upon a lotus flower in a meditative mood. It is also believed that his monk's robe is a special garment made from the silky fiber of the lotus stem. Thus, in the East, the lotus is often associated with purity, peace and reverence.

At Inle Lake in the Shan State of upper Myanmar, this ancient and fine tradition of producing rare fabric from lotus silk has been maintained to this day. Nang is a third generation successor of her family's workshop which began in 1932, from a modest beginning of ten looms to now with over 100 looms. While reeling and weaving of regular silk continues to be their main business, the most proud and valued product is their lotus silk scarf.

奧地利客人，都來 *Nang* 這裡尋找這種珍貴的布料。眼光獨特的觀光客也會挑這純手工製的蓮花圍巾當紀念品或是禮物。

Loro Piana 是第五代的義大利布料商，只販賣最好的布料，他們出版了一本非常精緻的書，裡面介紹這種很特別的、用蓮花莖抽取的絲所織成的布和利用這種布作出的產品。首次和這塊布料相遇的那一刻，*Loro Piana* 的老闆兄弟就決定要去茵萊湖尋找這塊布的源頭。他們對這工藝的讚賞佔去了這本書的好多頁。一件他們家品牌的披肩要價三千，一塊布料五千，一件量身訂做的夾克要一萬兩千，這可不是 *Kyat*，而是美金。

這種織布的方式其實非常複雜也很費工。製造一條絲巾需要六到八千根蓮花的莖，也就是說採收的面積超過一英畝。採收的時間只有從六月到十月，要讓莖生長到夠長才能採收。從採收原料，到製成夠做一條絲巾的纖維，需要一個人花二十天的時間，這段時間內還要小心翼翼的用手取材以及紡織這種細緻的纖維。編織跟染色要再花上另外四天。

我第一次被邀請去晉見達賴喇嘛時，我們在他在 *Dharamsala* 的住所單獨會面，我獻上這款罕見的絲巾，那是他最喜歡的藏橘紅色，也是最傳統活佛用的顏色。接

Today, monks as far away as Japan and choicest customers from France, Germany and Austria continue to seek for this priced fabric coming out of the House of Nang. Tourists with discerning taste also choose this exceptional all hand-made product as souvenir or gift.

It is not by coincidence that Loro Piana, the Italian house with a five-generation heritage of the finest fabric, published a coffee-table book in praise of lotus silk and offers products produced from this unique material, unlike any other. Upon touching this fiber for the first time, Sergio and Pier Luigi

到手上後，他馬上將絲巾捧起觸碰自己的額頭，並將絲巾擺掛在肩上。這是一種祝福的動作，這也是藏人的傳統，他們會獻上一種白色的絲巾哈達（*Khata*）以表祝福。可以肯定的是，這條取之不易的蓮花絲巾是最合適這位高僧的禮物了。

Exchanging lotus scarf with silk khata / 蓮花絲巾換來絲質哈達

Loro Piana were determined to make a pilgrimage to the magical Inle Lake to find out the source for themselves. Their words of praise filled pages of the colorful book. A shawl under its label sells for around 3,000, a piece of fabric 5,000, and a tailored jacket 12,000, not Kyat, but in US Dollars.

This unique and precious material is produced in an intricate and painstaking process. It takes six to eight thousand lotus flower stems to produce enough silk for one scarf, which must be harvested from more than one acre of the lotus pond. It can only be harvested between June and October, when the flower stalks have fully lengthened. From this raw material, it takes 20 days for one person to produce enough fiber for one scarf, carefully extracting and spinning the delicate fibers by hand. Weaving and dyeing take an additional 4 days.

Upon meeting the Dalai Lama for the first time, a private audience at his residence in Dharamsala, I offered His Holiness one of these rare scarves, in his favorite and traditional color, saffron orange. Immediately he touched the scarf upon his forehead, a gesture of blessing like he would do with the Tibetan traditional offering of white silk scarf called Khata, before setting it softly over his shoulder. Certainly this is a most appropriate gift for such important Buddhist high monk.

在馬尼拉的遭遇

MANILA ENCOUNTER

Manila, Philippines – December 18, 2015

在馬尼拉的遭遇

「你知道菲律賓需要什麼嗎？」*Sionil* 舒服地坐在椅子上問。「要什麼？」我回問。「一場革命！」*Sionil* 身體往餐桌靠近看著我，並舉起一隻手指來強調這論點。

一位九十一歲老人說出來的話聽起來很激進很挑釁，其他人在他這年紀不是已經進入天堂就是地獄，或是在這兩者中間，退休久了變得一點鬥志都沒有。但那絕不會是我們這位九十幾歲的先生，他因為敢於發表看法而聞名，他銳利的文字更是令人畏懼。

為此，他的護照在菲律賓獨裁前期多次被扣留。他書店廁所的外牆上掛著一支損壞折斷的西華（*Sheaffer*）鋼筆。筆框的下面寫著，他的書店／辦公室／家被竊盜洗劫一蹋糊塗時，這支筆遭受「特別」攻擊。沒有貴重東西被偷，事實上沒有一樣東西不見，只是他個人的檔案被翻過，被搞得一團糟。其他人有槍，*Sionil* 有筆，破壞他的筆代表拿走他的武器。

MANILA ENCOUNTER

"You know what the Philippines need?" asked Sionil while relaxing back on the lunch table chair. "What?" I queried. "A Revolution," Sionil leaned forward against the table and looked at me with a finger in the air to make his point.

Now, that is pretty radical and provocative for an old man of 91, when others his age would either be in heaven, purgatory, and if still in between, being long retired and have no more fighting spirit. But not so for this nonagenarian known for his vocal opinion, and more fearsome his sharp pen.

For that, he had his passport withheld several times during an earlier era when the Philippines was under dictatorial rule. On the wall right outside the toilet of his bookstore is a framed pen, a broken Sheaffer pen. Below is a description, remembering how this writing instrument was dealt an intentional blow when his bookstore/office/home was burglarized and ransacked. No valuable, in fact nothing, was lost. But his personal files were dug through, leaving a mess. Others may have guns, Sionil has his pen. Breaking his pen is a symbol of disarming him.

把筆弄壞，象徵的是對一位頭腦清晰，文字犀利的作者的一個警告，警告他不要再為社會上的不公與政府的貪腐發聲。*Sionil* 寫過多本得獎的書，好幾本被翻譯成二十幾國的語言。他雖然寫的多是小說，但是故事裡常諷刺菲律賓制度的敗壞跟社會上的問題。

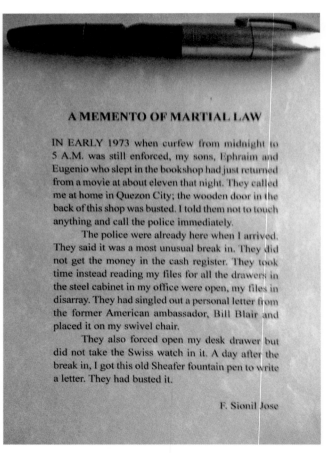

A MEMENTO OF MARTIAL LAW

IN EARLY 1973 when curfew from midnight to 5 A.M. was still enforced, my sons, Ephraim and Eugenio who slept in the bookshop had just returned from a movie at about eleven that night. They called me at home in Quezon City; the wooden door in the back of this shop was busted. I told them not to touch anything and call the police immediately.

The police were already here when I arrived. They said it was a most unusual break in. They did not get the money in the cash register. They took time instead reading my files for all the drawers in the steel cabinet in my office were open, my files in disarray. They had singled out a personal letter from the former American ambassador, Bill Blair and placed it on my swivel chair.

They also forced open my desk drawer but did not take the Swiss watch in it. A day after the break in, I got this old Sheafer fountain pen to write a letter. They had busted it.

F. Sionil Jose

Broken Sheaffer pen / 被折斷的西華鋼筆

The broken pen served as warning to a lucid and articulating writer, someone who has opined against social injustice and a corrupt government. Sionil had written numerous award-winning books, some translated into over 20 languages. Though he writes mainly novels, his books often satirize and reflect the decaying system and social ills of his country.

My visit, including a lunch at the Kashmir Restaurant a few steps away from Sionil's bookstore, was set up by Eddie Jose, his son who has become a close friend though we met only a few months ago. Eddie is a master restorer of oriental scroll painting and Thangka, having studied under a Japanese master for twelve years. Eddie now splits his time between the US, the world at large, and Bhutan where he devotes several months a year to teach Buddhist monks the art of restoration at a Center he created.

My meeting with the father Jose however was a bit more dramatic. Just a day ago I delivered a dinner lecture at the posh Tower Club to the World Presidents' Organization (WPO) Chapter in Manila. Upon leaving the venue in an elevator, a guest asked what I would do in Manila. I answered that I'll be visiting Sionil Jose, the writer. One lady in the elevator responded with a sour face, "but he is known to dislike Chinese." I was a bit taken by surprise, but readily retorted, "But I am sure he likes Chinese food".

In fact our meeting was most amicable, thanks perhaps to his son's

我的拜訪，還包括一頓在 *Kashmir Restaurant* 的午餐，餐廳離 *Sionil* 的書店只有幾步路，飯局是由他的兒子 *Eddie* 安排的，我幾個月前第一次見到 *Eddie* 面後，就跟他變成很好的朋友。*Eddie* 是東方卷軸畫跟唐卡的頂尖修復師，跟著日本大師學習了十二年。*Eddie* 現在的生活中心在美國，但也常常出差到世界各地，每年他都會花幾個月的時間在不丹，他創辦的中心教導和尚們修復唐卡方面的工藝。

與他父親的見面有點戲劇性。前一天我受邀到世界領袖組織（*World President's Organization*）馬尼拉分會演講，那是在一個很棒的 *Tower Club* 裡。就在正要離開的時候，電梯裡一位客人問我會在馬尼拉做些什麼事。我回答說我會去見作家 *Sionil Jose*。一位女士面有難色的說「他討厭中國人可是出了名的呵。」我有點吃驚，但又馬上回嘴「但我認為他一定喜歡中國菜」。

事實上我們的見面很愉快，也許是因為他兒子介紹我也是個作家。「我 1965 年開始經營這家書店，」他跟我說，書店的名字是 *Solidaridad*，會選擇這樣的名字顯示他是有階級意識的。書架上有許多關於亞洲各國的選書。比例上中國佔了很大的一部分，還有一些比較有爭議的或是較「另類」的書，也有些甚至我都不知道的書，我之前還以為我對關於中國的書算是閱讀廣泛的。

introduction that I too, am a writer. "I started this bookstore in 1965," he explained to me. Solidaridad is the name. That choice of name put Sionil into a class of consciousness. The shelves have many select books on various subjects about countries of Asia. Proportionally China has a very large section, including some of the more controversial or "alternative" books that I am not even aware of, though I consider myself an avid reader of books on China.

On the second floor is the office. Third floor is Sionil's "home" with a round table and a small rectangular one. "For long years, writers often gather here around my table," he confided to me. In one corner is his work desk, with many books and a bookshelf to the side. A half open curtain, imprinted with pattern of a bookshelf, veiled off his bed right next to his desk.

"I still enjoy writing by hand, using a pen, though I have this old typewriter," Sionil regaled as he pointed to an electric typewriter sitting behind him over the window counter. He then showed me his diary. I turned to one page and saw an entry from some years ago. His handwriting, or penmanship should I say, is superb and very legible. One paragraph written in blue ink mentioned that he would love to visit Japan where his son Eddie apprenticed.

Our conversation covered a wide range of subjects, politics, art, and history of his two years spent living in Hong Kong as an editor for a magazine. He did at one point mentioned about us Chinese; that the newly arrived Chinese

書店的二樓是辦公室，三樓是 Sionil 的「家」，有一張圓桌跟一張小的長桌。「多年來，作家們常常在這裡聚會。」他對我傾訴。其中一個角落擺放著他的書桌，桌上放了很多書，書桌旁有個書架。房間的窗簾拉開一半，上面印著書架的圖案，後面是他的床，緊鄰著書桌。

「我還是很享受用筆書寫，即使我也有一台老舊的打字機……」Sionil 很高興地指著一台靠窗的電子打字機，然後他給我看他的日記。我慢慢地翻到一頁多年前寫的，我必須說他的手寫字或是筆觸真是好看，非常清晰。其中有一段用藍色墨水的文字寫到他很想去日本一趟，看看他兒子 Eddie 實習的地方。

我們聊了很多，話題包括政治，藝術。他說，他也在香港住過兩年，當一個雜誌的編輯。聊天時他的確提到了我們中國人，他說如果中國與菲律賓的敵意增高的時候，這些新來的中國移民一定會心向中國；但是他又將幾代前就移民到菲律賓的中國人劃分出來，感覺他們會效忠菲律賓。

我買了很多關於菲律賓的書，幾本是關於中國的。道別的時候 Sionil 選了兩本書簽名送給我。《Sherds》這本比較薄，關於一個中國來菲律賓的第四代移民，是位陶藝教授，繼承了很多財產跟房產，在柏克萊大學取得博士後回到菲律賓教書。藝術學院的院長是個女的，也是從柏克萊

probably would pledge allegiance to China if hostility between the Philippines and China were to flare up. He however did distinguish those who had made the country their home for generations, feeling that they would be loyal to the Philippines.

I bought many books, mostly on the Philippines and a few on China. As a parting gift, Sionil signed two books of his choice to me. Sherds, the thinner of the two, was about a fourth generation Chinese pottery professor who inherited huge wealth and multiple homes, returning to teach at the university after acquiring his PhD from UC-Berkeley. The Dean of the Art School is a woman who also returned from Berkeley.

For a novel written when Sionil was well into his eighties, the romance and suspense read like from the pen of someone still with passion in surplus, including some rather suggestive description courtship and bedroom encounters. Charting the high-style comfortable life around the globe of PG the potter, at times into great detail of these destinations and daily trivials, the story unveils with many surprises.

The vivid depiction of the polarity between a well-heeled Chinese's attempt to mentor a destitute student from a dilapidated village outside the city, moving into the slump of Manila while pursuing her education, was a plot which further fortified Sionil's life-long conviction about the precipice between the

回來的。

Sionil 這本在八十幾歲的時候寫的小說，浪漫、懸疑的情節好像是出自一位充滿熱情的人，裡面對情愛也有相當露骨的描寫。*PG* 是位陶藝家，生活過得很好，很舒服，世界遊走，有些時候對於一些地點有詳細的描述，也有日常生活裡瑣碎的小事，隨著故事的發展也慢慢揭開許多驚喜。

故事生動地描寫著一位富有的中國人，試圖去指導來自城外荒村的貧窮學生，這個學生為了可以受更好的教育而搬到馬尼拉城市內的貧民窟。這是故事的大概，裡面 *Sionil* 除了加入他一輩子所相信的真理以外，也一貫地為社會底層發聲。

道別時我並不覺得 *Sionil* 排斥中國人，在他簽給我的書上寫著「我希望你近期內還會回來這裡」。

同一天的晚上，我受邀去一個朋友的家裡用餐，*Albert del Rosario*（菲律賓外交部部長）也是座上賓。我想菲律賓的外交部長很可能會對中國人沒什麼善意，因為最近在南沙群島發生的事件。但意外的，晚餐前後我們有機會聊上天，並且很愉快。

他說他下午才去見艾奎諾總統，跟他報告 *BBC* 播報的新聞，關於中國漁民在南沙群島海底拖網，造成珊瑚礁很大

Sionil with HM inside bookstoren / 作者和 Sionil 在書店內

have and the have-not.

We parted way as I realized that Sionil is not against all Chinese after all. On the page he signed his book for me, he penned that he hope I will soon come back!

That same evening, I was invited to a home dinner which Albert del Rosario also attended. As Secretary of Foreign Affairs for the Philippines, here is another gentleman who would likely have an unfavorable attitude toward a Chinese, given the current impasse over the Spratly with China. But instead, we had a cheerful chat before and after dinner.

He recounted that he just saw President Aquino the same afternoon,

的損害。因為外交不是我的專長，我只是靜靜地聆聽，沒有表示贊同或是不贊同。

因為美國的大使 Philip Goldberg 跟澳洲大使 Bill Twiddell 都在這場私人晚宴，我很想問菲律賓政府會不會跟美國抗議他們的空軍跟驅逐艦進入南沙群島，那可是菲律賓宣稱的領土，以及會不會對澳洲的軍機也一併抗議。

猶豫一下，還是忍住不要問這樣敏感的問題。畢竟外交部長在，我應該要禮貌點，才不會被這國家列入不受歡迎的名單。我也不可以像九十一歲的 Sionil 那樣挑釁。不過我提到了學會在巴拉望，靠近南沙群島做的工作，包括研究跟保育珊瑚礁的魚類；還有，這裡的魚，可是香港人很喜愛的美饌呢。

晚宴結束前大家一起拍團體照，外交部長走過來站在我旁邊。他把手摟住我的肩膀，我突然覺得也許 Sionil Jose 或是 Albert del Rasario 說的話也只是有一定時限的。希望歷史會站在我這邊。

reporting to him the BBC story about Chinese fishermen around the Spratly dredging the bottom of the sea, thus damaging much of the coral. As I am no foreign policy or diplomatic expert, I could only listen without concurring or disagreeing.

Since both Ambassador Philip Goldberg of the U.S. and Ambassador Bill Twiddell of Australia were present at this private dinner, I was tempted to ask whether the Philippine government protested the transgression of US Airforce planes and destroyer over his country's claimed territory of the Spratly, likewise the Australian military plane.

But I hesitated and restrained myself in raising such sensitive question. After all, with the Foreign Minister, I ought to be diplomatic rather than being considered a person non grata while visiting his country. Nor can I be provocative like 91-years-vintage Sionil. But I did mention briefly that our Society's efforts in Palawan near the Spratly include trying to study and protect the coral fish, a diet of delicacy to those of us in Hong Kong.

As our dinner party rose to take a group photo before leaving, the Foreign Minister cozy up and stood next to me. With his one arm around my shoulder, I suddenly felt that perhaps all the rhetoric, be it from Sionil Jose or Albert del Rosario, are just for the time being. Hopefully history will bear me out on this!

Minister Rosario standing next to HM /
作者與眾友人合照。右一為菲律賓外交部長 Albert del Rosario 先生

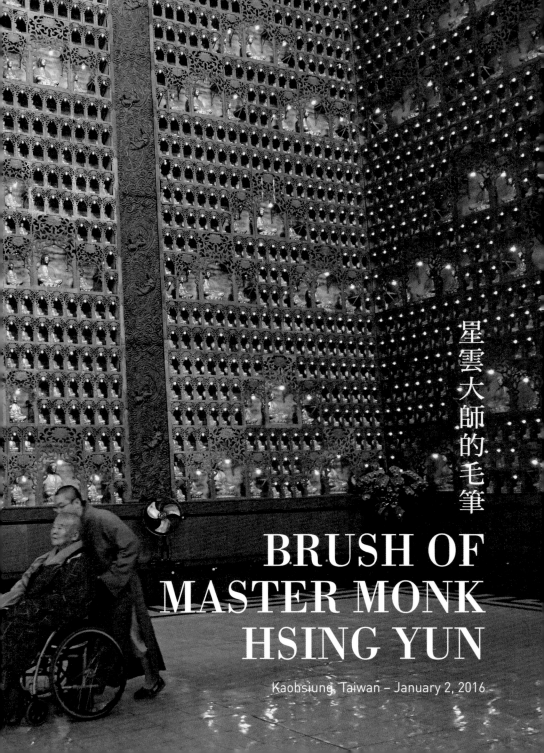

星雲大師的毛筆

BRUSH OF MASTER MONK HSING YUN

Kaohsiung, Taiwan – January 2, 2016

星雲大師的毛筆

「我如果寫一個字就停下來的話,我就不知道下一個字要從哪裡開始……」大師用溫和帶點沙啞的聲音說著。他跟我解釋為什麼他一下筆的時候就會連續寫上好幾個字,或是一句話。因為如果不這樣的話,字就不會成一行直線。他的書法是以「一氣呵成」聞名的。

星雲大師今年九十歲,幾乎都看不到了,長久以來的糖尿病把他困在輪椅上。視力雖然很差,但其他一切的功能都很好,尤其是他的大腦。大家都說大師是用他的心去書寫。與他早期寫的字相比,真的,現在的更老練,更流暢,筆觸充滿生命跟力道。

寫書法已經變成他每天要做的事,也是他的運動。他的書法受到信徒極大的歡迎,贏得很高的評價,跟價錢,因為贊助者會拿錢出來捐贈給大師創的文化教育基金會。「我的基金會現在有十八億,我想應該可以成長到五十億」大師告訴我。

BRUSH OF MASTER MONK HSING YUN

"If I stop my writing at one word, I won't know where to begin with the next one," the monk said with a soft and coarse voice. *He was trying to explain to me why all his writings, at times a few words or up to a phrase or a sentence, must be completed within the same stroke of the brush. Otherwise the words would not be aligned perfectly in a vertical line. His calligraphy has now become famously known as the "One Stroke Script".*

Monk Hsing Yun, turning 90 this year, is clinically blind, as well as confined to a wheelchair, due largely to a long history of diabetes. Blind only in sight, certainly not with his other faculties, be that his mind or his heart. As others all say and attest to, the monk writes with his heart. Compare to his earlier writings, indeed today's script is far more seasoned and expressive, the brush stroke, full of power and vigor.

Chinese brush writing has become his daily routine and exercise. These scripts became much in demand by his followers, fetching high praises, as well as price, as supplicants pour out their pocket to help fill a foundation the monk has created to benefit culture and education. "My foundation now has over

他說的是新台幣，用來支持文化跟教育。「不過我從不碰錢，完全由基金會自己裁量要怎麼運用。」他又說。以現在的匯率，十八億大約是美金五千四百七十萬。

我再次到佛光山來拍大師寫字，非常大的佛教園區，坐落在高雄。2014 年我很榮幸的當上這寺廟的駐寺攝影藝術家，我跟星雲大師說我會專注在紀錄他的書法。因為他所到之處都會有相機拍他，不管在台灣，中國大陸，甚至是世界各地。

要拍他寫書法的話，就得要到他居住的地方，他的起居室，這樣親密的環境讓我可以近距離的觀察他。這不僅可以滿足我自己的興趣，也讓我有所收穫，拍攝他的同時我也得到幾幅他寫的珍貴書法。

要拍攝他並不容易，得考慮他的健康跟體力，再加上我自己的行程也排得很滿。上一次我來的時候住在紫竹林，一個很棒很安靜的別墅，專為接待貴賓所蓋的；不過我並沒有見到他，因為醫生要他住院。

不過他的精神狀況還是非常好的。光是 2015 年他就寫了兩本書，只是現在他只能將他要寫下來的文字說出來，由工作人員記下來。他為報紙專欄寫了七十篇文章，描述台灣今年一月選舉期間的政治問題，用的是＜趙無任＞這

1.8 billion, and I think it can grow to 5 billion," the monk revealed to me.

He was referring to the capital they have raised in Taiwanese Dollars, for the sake of supporting education and culture. "But I never touch any of the money, it is fully under the discretion of the foundation to disperse it," he further qualified. At current rate, 1.8 billion is equivalent to approximately 54.7 million USD.

I have come again to Fo Guang Shan, the massive Buddhist Temple compound in Kaohsiung of Taiwan, to photograph the monk's writing. After being honored as the Resident Photographic Artist of the Temple in 2014, I told the Master Monk Hsing Yun that I would only focus on documenting his writing. He has been photographed everywhere he went, be it in Taiwan, Mainland China, or all over the world.

To concentrate on his calligraphy would take me into his inner sanctuary, his living quarters and his living room. Such intimate coverage would allow me to gain access and observe him close up. It would also satisfy my self interest, or complementary interest should I say, in photographing him while acquiring some of his prized calligraphy.

But even that is not easily accomplished, due to my own tight schedule of travels, as well as the monk's declining health and energy. On my previous

個筆名。深廣的知識，引述的歷史，文學與詩；對於時事的見解真是令人震驚。

當作者的身分揭曉時，大家都很吃驚。最後文章被集結出版成書，星雲大師以第三人的姿態為書寫序，讓趙無任這個人代表全台灣的每個人。

他另外一本書的啟發是源自社會突然對佛教團體的批評。在＜貧僧有話要說＞ 這本書裡面他駁斥對宗教團體不公平的批評，他也特別提到佛光山的歷史跟一些大家不知道的故事，其間他與信徒克服無數的困難才讓佛光山有今天的樣貌。整個過程他將功勞歸於他的同事與支持者，完全地展現他的謙卑和謙遜。

我在十二月三十一日抵達，被告知星雲大師的右手發炎有些腫，因為前一天書寫太久了。醫生命令他的右手必需要休息。我可以理解為什麼，因為大師用的筆很大支很重。寫大字的時候，他的手必須要懸空，沒法子靠在桌子上。這樣的筆鋒需要力道，以他的年紀來說是相當吃力的。

接待我的阿尼以為我一定會非常失望，我調侃的說這一定是個好預兆，讓我一定得要再回來這裡。我也剛好遇上跨年的煙火，迎接二零一六年的到來。他們跟我說一月一日早上九點半，會有一百對的新人在佛光山舉行婚禮，其中

trip, he was kept in the hospital by his doctor and we failed to meet as I waited at "Zi Zhu Lin" (Purple Bamboo Forest), a nice and quiet villa he created for special guests.

His mental condition, however, is still most vibrant. Within 2015 alone, he has authored two major volumes, though these days he would dictate his intended writing to his staff. Using a pseudo name of Zhao Wu-ren, he wrote a newspaper column totaling 70 articles, depicting the ills of Taiwan's current political situation during the run up to the election this January. The breadth of knowledge and citation of history, literature and poems, as well as regarding current affairs and situation was mindboggling.

When it was revealed that the author was actually the famous monk, everyone was surprised. Eventually the articles were published as a book, with Monk Hsing Yun writing the Foreword in the third person, assigning the author Chao as representing everyone in Taiwan.

His other book was inspired by the sudden flare up of criticism on Buddhist groups of Taiwan. Titled Poor Monk Has Something To Say, he rebutted the unfair criticism on such religious groups, in particular recounting the long history and hidden stories of his own organization. This became a record of the difficulties he and his followers had to undergo in order to take Fo Guang Shan to where it is today. In the process, he gave credit by name to many of

還包括來自中國大陸與香港的新人。

還有許多結婚四十、五十、甚至六十年的夫妻也來參加，當作是慶祝他們的紅寶石婚、金婚，與鑽石婚。大約有一千對的新人，之前可能因為貧窮、戰爭或是種種的原因結了婚沒有行禮的，今天也來了。大師親自主持婚禮，給予年輕與年長的夫妻祝福。

不到八點我突然被阿尼告知星雲大師想要在八點半，典禮還沒開始的時候，在他的住所跟我見面，於是我們很快地離開我住的別墅開車抵達大師住的地方。我被帶到他家，這裡我曾經來過，在客廳裡我們互相問候，聊了一下。不一會兒我被帶到他的房間，裡面有一張長桌，同時

Diamond anniversary couples / 鑽石婚的老夫妻

his associates and supporters. His modesty and humility is fully represented in this work.

The day I arrived, on December 31, I was told that Monk Hsing Yun's right arm has become swollen and inflamed, having been writing for too long the previous day. His arm was grounded, by the doctor. I could well understand the predicament as he writes with a big brush. While writing these large scripts, he could not rest his hand on the table and must keep it lifted in mid air. At the same time, such strokes require rigor and force, an immense strain on the energy of someone his age.

The nuns attending to me thought I must be hugely disappointed. I quipped

Bride and groom / 新娘與新郎

是他的餐桌、會議桌、工作桌，當然也是寫書法的桌子。綠色絲絨上面擺著紙墨，但這只是擺飾。不過為了不讓我失望，大師決定裝模作樣好像他正在寫書法，好來滿足我的期待，讓我能夠拍攝他正在書寫的樣子。這雖然不是最好的狀況，但是我還是拍了，我跟他承諾當他的手好的時候我會再回來。道別的時候他送給了我一對我剛拍的書法。

接下來我去參觀集團婚禮，觀看大師主持這個的典禮。第三天我要離開的時候阿尼帶來大師送給我的禮物。他送給了我一對用過的毛筆，大的是寫書法用的，小的是簽名用的。我非常珍惜它們，現在我可以把它們跟之前大師給我

that the situation must be a good omen for me to come back again. In the mean time, I was able to enjoy the display of fireworks as the clock hit 12 midnight as we welcome the arrival of 2016. January 1 and New Year was just around the corner. I was told that at 9:30, one hundred couples would be getting married at Fo Guang Shan at a mass wedding ceremony, including even couples from Mainland China and Hong Kong.

Many other senior couples attending the event have been married for 40, 50 or even 60 years. They would also attend as they would be celebrating their Ruby, Golden and Diamond wedding anniversary. About 1000 couples, who in earlier days due to poverty, war or whatever reasons, could not be officially married, would also be present as wedded couples. The Monk would appear to officiate and bless the new and old couples.

Before 8 a.m. however, I was suddenly summoned by the nuns, announcing that Monk Hsing Yun would like to see me at his home at 8:30, before the ceremony would begin. We quickly left my villa and drove to the old residence of the Monk. There I was escorted to his home, which I had visited on earlier trips. Ushered into a sitting room, we greeted each other and chatted. Before long, I was led into his bed room where his long table serves as dining, meeting, working and calligraphy table.

On a green velvet top, paper and ink were all prepared. These however,

的書法擺在一起了。

我的拜訪很短暫，這三天來我都吃素。可是我那世俗的胃
要求要有些變化。很特別的機會讓我在一個很重要的寺廟
度過我的新年，與一位被敬重的大師一起。相信這對我跟
CERS 來說會是個新年的好兆頭，對我的親友們也如是。

Fireworks over Fo Guang Shan / 佛光山的煙火

were all for show. In order not to disappoint me totally, the honorable monk decided to act out as if writing, so as to satiate my desire to photograph him in the act. While this is not perfect rendering of his calligraphy, I had to settle with this, and promised him that I would return soon, when his arm would be well and his writing resumed. As a parting gift, he gave me that pair of long script I was photographing.

For the rest of the day, I was able to participate in the wedding ceremony, and observed the Monk in officiating the event. Just before my departure on the third day, the nuns brought to my villa yet another parting gift from Monk Hsing Yun. He had sent over a pair of worn brush, one large one for calligraphy, and the other smaller, for signing his name. I prized such specimens as they can now be displayed along his other calligraphy that he had given me before.

While my visit was short, by now I have had three days of strictly vegetarian meals. My secular stomach is calling for a change. It had been very special that I passed my New Year at an important Buddhist Temple, and with audience of a very senior and honorable monk. Perhaps this would usher in a good year, for me and CERS, as well as for all my friends and relatives.

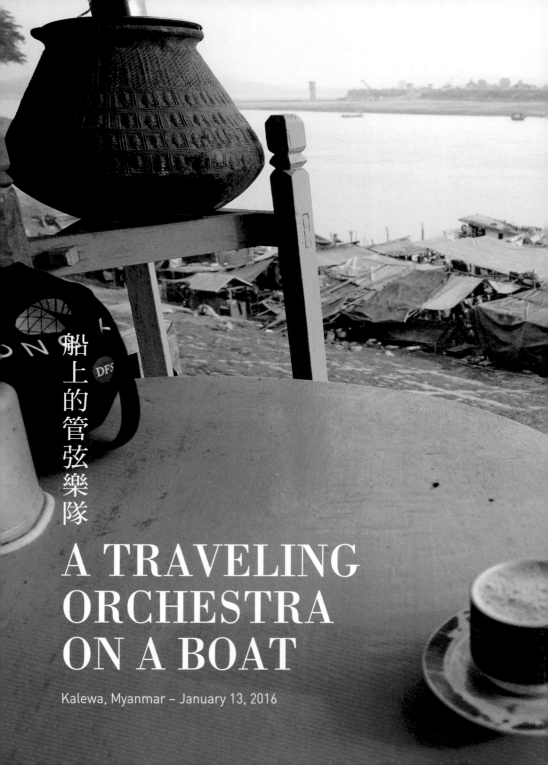

船上的管弦樂隊

A TRAVELING ORCHESTRA ON A BOAT

Kalewa, Myanmar – January 13, 2016

船上的管弦樂隊

音樂的節奏跟著兩組鼓聲還有大小不一的鑼鳴，還有鈸跟一個高音的管樂器叫 *Hnal*，突然間節奏加快，音樂聲漸漸加強。此刻 *Ko Thant Sin* 開始唱歌。

歌詞因為是緬甸語所以我聽不懂，但是從他臉上的表情可以感受得到歌裡的情感。這首歌裡放進很多感情，讓我感覺好像在美國的南部聽著混著爵士的藍調。這裡的旋律跟美國的是非常不同的。

當 *Thant Sin* 唱歌的時候他的手動的很快，像在畫圓，敲打著鼓，大大小小的鼓圍繞著他，從前到後。主唱跟 *Thant Sin* 管樂隊的隊長正在表演一首很受歡迎的歌叫「亞洲英雄」，是獻給緬甸現代史上最受尊敬的翁山將軍的一首歌，這位翁山將軍就是翁山蘇姬的父親。通常這首歌是在觀眾的情緒漲到最高的時候才拿出來唱，隨後樂團會再表演幾首歌來結束這場演唱會。這首歌長達七分鐘，一首非常消耗體力的歌。

A TRAVELING ORCHESTRA ON A BOAT

The tempo of music, set to instruments including two sets of drums, a score of variation sizes of gongs, accompanied by cymbals and a high pitch wind instrument called Hnal suddenly went much faster, as if reaching a crescendo. Momentarily Ko Thant Sin's vocal for the song started.

The lyrics, being in Burmese and unintelligible to me, nonetheless seemed to come alive through his facial expressions. A lot of emotions were put into this rendition of a song that I felt like being in the southern USA, listening to some kind of blues mixed with jazz. The rhythms however are very different.

While Thant Sin was singing, his hands moved in a dramatic fast circular motion, beating on a roll of drums, may be twenty or more in various sizes, surrounding him literally from front to back. The lead singer and leader of the Thant Sin Orchestra was performing a popular song called Asian Hero, a tribute to the most revered figure in modern Myanmar history, General Aung San, father of Aung San Suu Kyi. Usually this special number is reserved for the height of their performance, when the audience would also get into a spell of excitement, before the orchestra would gradually play out other numbers

我乘著 HM Explorer 在欽敦江已經三天了，剛好遇到這個流動的樂團，他們也是以船做交通工具。我第一次短暫的遇見他們是在兩年前，當時我們研究用的船剛剛正式啟用，自從那時候開始我就很想要回來紀錄他們的故事。

我們很幸運的在他們常駐的基地 Kalewa 遇見他們，那裏離印度邊境的 Tamu 很近，二戰時英國軍隊曾在這裡進行大規模撤退。當有宗教儀式或慶典舉行時，這些流動的音樂家就會受邀去表演，娛樂大眾的同時，主人也會為了蓋寺廟和佛塔或是為了修繕而募款。偶爾他們也會受邀到私人的聚會表演，比如婚禮。

這種移動的樂隊有悠久的歷史，也是屬於這條河的一部分。由於沿著河岸的道路陸續鋪設了起來，河裡往來的船隻也開始漸漸減少了。拜這國家這幾年對外開放所賜，鄉村也變得繁榮了；信徒蓋的寺廟與佛塔也越蓋越多，這讓樂團很忙碌，一年可以接到三十到四十場的宗教儀式、各類慶典以及民間活動的邀約。

這個流動樂團的行業從 Thant Sin 的祖父就開始了，看起來不久後第四代也會接下棒子，因為 Ko 的女兒還不到十歲，就已經加緊腳步參與這個樂團了。下課後 Moh Moh 會跟著樂團，就像今天，她已經可以隨著樂團的伴奏演唱了，當父親的當然是很驕傲。在臨時搭建的舞台後面有一

to end the show. This particular piece would last for seven minutes, a rather exhausting performance.

I have been traveling up the Chindwin River on our HM Explorer boat for three days, just to catch up with this other traveling orchestra, also on a boat. I first ran into this orchestra briefly over two years ago, soon after we launched our own research vessel in Myanmar. Since then, I've been eager to return and document their story.

We were lucky to catch them at their home base of Kalewa, a short distance from the Indian border of Tamu where a massive retreat of British forces took place during World War Two. As a traveling minstrel, the troupe is called in to perform during religious functions or festivities, to entertain while the host would collect donations for the many temples and pagodas being built, or needing repair and restoration. Occasionally they would also perform at private functions, like at weddings.

Such traveling orchestra has a long history and is part of a tradition along the river. With new roads now being built along the banks, river traffic may gradually trickle down. Luckily the countryside has become more prosperous due to opening up of the country in the last few years. More and more temples, as well as pagodas, are being put up by supplicants. Such activities keep the troupe busy, being invited to perform 30 to 40 times a year at

張 *Moh Moh* 的大海報，旁邊那張就是 *Ko* 自己的。在河岸旁用竹子搭起棚子，以棕櫚葉做屋頂，就成了他們練習的「工作室」，裡面勉強可以容納六位客人。

其實 *Thant Sin* 並不是跟他的父親或是祖父學藝，而是跟著一個叫「*Sein Hla Sin*」的樂團。他從九歲就開始跟著那個樂團，兩年的實習時間裡，沒有薪水可拿，每天只有兩餐，鋪個墊子就睡在船上。很自然地，他的女兒 *Moh Moh* 也是在九歲開始習藝，不過她同時也在上學，

religious ceremonies, festivals and civil events.

For Thant Sin and his family, playing in a traveling orchestra has gone on for three generations, since his grandfather's day. Soon, it seems set to move to a fourth generation as Ko's daughter, barely ten years old, is quickening her step to get involved with the orchestra. Today, or any other day after school, Moh Moh can hold her own with her singing to the accompaniment of the orchestra. The father is obviously proud, as a huge poster of Moh Moh is hung behind a make-shift stage, next to Ko's poster of himself. This bamboo shed with palm-leaf roof by the bank serves as their rehearsal "studio", but with barely enough space to sit at most half a dozen guests.

Thant Sin began learning the art of such performance as a young apprentice, not from his father or grandfather, but from another troupe "Sein Hla Sin". For two years since nine years old, he stayed with this troupe without pay, just two meals a day and a mat to sleep on a boat. So it seems natural that his daughter Moh Moh should also start learning at nine, while attending school at the same time. Education is considered very important to any Burmese, thus Moh Moh's singing can only be done after school.

Today Thant Sin is 40 years old. He was formerly known as Zaw Min Hlaing, and was little known to anyone at that time. In 2006, he met the monk Sayar Taw Wai Zayantar. The monk gave him a new name Thant Sin to bring more

Moh with her mom / Moh 和母親

緬甸人非常重視教育，所以 Moh Moh 只能在下課後才能去唱歌。

今年 Thant Sin 四十歲。他之前叫 Zaw Min Hlaing，但是知道他的人不多。二零零六年他遇見一位叫 Sayar Taw Wai Zayantar 的和尚，和尚給了他 Thant Sin 這名字，說這名字會帶給他幸運與名氣。看起來新名字果然有用，二零零八年他用自己的名字創辦了自己的樂團。他們的樂團突然間變的很受歡迎，邀約不斷。

Thant Sin 的管樂隊現在有八個成員，大多是家人組成的，Thant Sin 四十三歲的哥哥 Aung Khaing Min 會所有的樂器，三十歲的妹妹 Nwe Ni Hlaing 唱歌，六十七歲的父親 U San Hlaing 吹長笛跟一種像長笛的樂器。其他的成員還有一位三十歲的女歌手 Mya Mya Win，四十七歲的 U Maw Gyee 也是從九歲開始學藝，在二零一零年加入，而現在十八歲的 Thit Lwin Aung，他在十歲時開始實習，兩年後正式成為 Thant Sin 樂團的一員。

Moh Moh 雖然是個歌唱的天才，但是有時候還是會破音，聲音也常常被樂隊蓋過，不過 Thant Sin 預估她會愈唱愈好，希望屆時這流動樂隊的傳統還存在。既然樂團這幾個禮拜沒有受邀去表演，我邀請他們上來我們的探險船，在下午跟晚餐後表演。折疊式的舞台跟裝飾很快的搭起

luck and fame in the future. It seemed to have worked and he founded his own orchestra under his name in 2008. Their orchestra suddenly became popular and more in demand.

Thant Sin Orchestra now has eight members and is by and large a family minstrel, including Thant Sin's 43-years-old brother Aung Khaing Min who can also play all the instruments, younger sister at 30 Nwe Ni Hlaing who sings, their father U San Hlaing at 67 years of age who plays the flute and the "flute like wind". The other members include female singer Mya Mya Win (30), U Maw Gyee (47) who also started learning at age 9 and joined their troupe in 2010, and Thit Lwin Aung (18) who apprenticed for two years since age 10 before joining Thant Sin.

For Moh Moh, the child prodigy as a singer, her voice is still breaking and often drowned out by the orchestra. But as Thant Sin expected, in time she would excel as she grew older, hopefully before such traveling orchestras become obsolete. Since they are not receiving any order to perform these couple weeks, I invited the troupe on our boat to perform in the afternoon and after dinner. The collapsible stage and decorative enclosure were quickly set up, and we gave up our usual happy hour and instead enjoyed their performance. All our boat staff seemed to know many of the songs, either singing along or strumming their hands or feet in unison with the beat.

來，我們今天下午沒有平日的 *Happy Hour*，今天 *happy hour* 時段我們用來觀賞他們的表演。船上的工作人員好像都知道這些歌，不時跟著樂團一起唱，及就用手、腳一起打拍子。

此刻的緬甸北部正值冬天，樂團的親友們也上到我們的船觀看表演，在上層甲板緊抓著毛毯取暖。我答應他們我們還會回來紀錄他們到處表演的故事。

Kalewa 往上有個渡船口，上面有一家路邊的咖啡店，我坐下點了杯緬甸奶茶。在這個渡船口有許多小船載著村民去早市，也同樣在這裡，有大船載卡車跟汽車渡河。坐在船上的乘客每個人要付三百 *Kyat*，如果是坐運車渡輪就免費。但是時間寶貴，沒什麼人願搭免費的船。這跡象也顯示這個步調緩慢的國家開始有了變化。

再往遠一點的地方看過去，我看到一座橫跨欽敦江的大橋

More drums and cymbal / Moh Moh dancing / Moh Moh absorbed in singing

While this is winter in northern Myanmar, relatives and friends of the orchestra joined us on our boat as spectators, hugging their blanket on our upper deck benches. I promise that we would return another time, in order to document them traveling to various performances.

Nearby above Kalewa, I sit and enjoy my Burmese milk tea at a roadside cafe above the ferry crossing. I observe the many small boats busily ferrying villagers back and forth across the river to the morning market. Larger boats are ferrying trucks and cars across at the same location. It costs 300 Kyat for a passenger on the boat whereas if one were to wait for the vehicular ferry, the crossing is free. However time is of essence and it seems there is hardly any taker for the free ride. Such may be an indication of life ahead in an otherwise slow moving country.

As I look a little further into the distant, I can see that foundations are being laid across the Chindwin River for the construction of a major bridge.

大鼓和鈸 / Moh Moh 在跳舞 / Moh Moh 沉醉在歌唱裡

正在打基石。一旦這橋蓋好之後，這裡沿岸的咖啡店，餐廳，商店會逐漸消失。到時候乘車的人們忙碌地過著他們的生活，再也不會在等船的時候喝上一杯咖啡。

老朋友跟顧客隨著緬甸的進步成為過往的回憶。至於 Thant Sin 的樂隊，年輕一輩的娛樂除了電視還有手機的社群軟體，不知道還會不會去聽樂隊的表演。也許這也是我在這咖啡店最後的一杯茶，我在 Kalewa 渡船口最後的一眼。

Café overlooking ferryl / 渡船口旁的小吃店

Once this bridge is completed, all these cafes, restaurants and shops by the riverbank would become obsolete. Cars and passengers would hurry on with their life without stopping to enjoy a cup of tea while waiting for the ferry.

Old friends and customers may all become a passing memory as Myanmar rush to join the modern world. As with Thant Sin's traveling orchestra, he would be fortunate if the younger set of Burmese boys and girls would find time beyond their other choices on television program and social chatting over their now viral mobile phones. Perhaps this will also be my last cup of tea at this café, and my last look at the ferry crossing of Kalewa.

緬甸傳統陶藝的未來

FUTURE OF POTTERY TRADITION IN MYANMAR

Mandalay, Myanmar – January 19, 2016

緬甸傳統陶藝的未來

好幾艘小船被綁在岸邊，每艘都有木頭或竹子編的骨架。陶罐被倒過來堆疊在骨架內，有幾艘已經裝了半滿。這裡是欽敦江西岸的小村 *Kone Yin*，離南方的卡列瓦鎮有一段距離。沿著欽敦江跟伊洛瓦底江有好幾個做陶的村莊，這兒是其中的一個村子。欽敦江慢慢匯流進伊洛瓦底江，就在曼德勒的下方處。

因為是旱季，村子聳於水平面約十米處的土堤上，離岸邊大概二百五十米的距離。村子下方的沙岸上有著用稻草做的環狀籬笆。在這裡燒陶壺的窯底下舖的是花生殼，樹皮夾在中間，陶壺上面再蓋上稻草，然後再用泥土封起來，封好後再挖幾個通氣孔。經過一天的烘烤，土陶罐才成為可以被使用的陶製品。村子裡大約有一百三十戶，幾乎家家都在做陶。「窯」的附近到處都是破碎的陶片，它們最後會被打碎成粉好再利用。

陶土的原料採自附近一段泥濘的岸邊。用牛車運一車土到村子裡要四個鐘頭，三千五百緬元。一台牛車一天可以運

FUTURE OF POTTERY TRADITION IN MYANMAR

A number of small boats are tied to the bank, each with a wood and bamboo framework on it. A couple of these boats are half loaded, with pottery jars piled upside down against each other inside the frame. This is Kone Yin Village on the west bank of the Chindwin River, some distance south of Kalewa. It is one of several pottery villages along the Chindwin as well as the Irrawaddy rivers, with the former river merging into the latter below Mandalay.

It is dry season and the village, rising above an earth bank some ten meters high, is around 250 meters from the edge of the sandy shore. Below the village and standing on the sand are round circular structures made with straw fences. Here are where the clay pots are fired off, with peanut shells at bottom, tree bark in between and straw above the pots and mud with some exhaust holes on top to seal them off. After a day of baking, the jars will turn into usable pottery. There are around 130 families in the village, almost all engaged in pottery making. Sherd pieces lie around these "furnaces". They would be pounded into powder and be used again.

兩趟。硬化的泥土會被敲打成小塊浸泡在水裡，等到軟化後才變成可以再使用的陶土。除了陶藝，村民們也靠務農來生活。

「我一天只能做三十件。」*Ma Shwe Ei* 邊說邊忙著做陶罐。她三十歲，家族好幾代都是做陶的。旁邊有個女孩操作著拉坯器具，這邊 *Ma* 的雙手不用幾分鐘就快速的把一堆陶土變成完美的圓形陶罐。在當地陶罐一件賣五百緬元，若是運到卡列瓦鎮或是卡里的市場，就會賣到兩千到兩千五百緬元，是好幾倍的價格。

之後，我們順著伊洛瓦底江前往曼德勒下方另一個製陶的村子 *Tha Pate Tan* 做調研。小村離瓦提河跟伊洛瓦底江的合流處不遠，這裡大概一半的人家都在做筒裙（像沙籠的裙子），另外一半製陶。

他們製作的陶有大有小，高度從二十公分到四十公分。一

Raw clay comes from a section of the muddy shore some distance away. It takes an ox cart four hours to deliver one load of clay to the village, costing 3500 Kyat. Each day one cart can bring two loads. The hardened earth would be pounded into smaller pieces before being soaked in water to soften it into usable clay. Villagers are also engaged in subsistence farming.

"I only make 30 pieces per day," said Ma Shwe Ei while busily making some jars. She is 30 years old and her family has been making pottery for generations. With another girl working the spindle, Ma's hands work the pile of clay into a perfectly rounded jar within minutes. Locally the jars are sold for about 500 Kyat a piece. When it reaches market at Kalewa or Kalay, it can fetch between 2,000 and 2,500 per jar, delivering multiple times in value.

Later on as we sailed to the Irrawaddy below Mandalay, we visited another pottery village. Tha Pate Tan Village is a short distance up the confluence of the Dote Hta Wati river with the Irrawaddy. Here perhaps half the families are engaged in weaving Longyi (sarong-like skirts) and the rest in pottery making.

Here they make vases big and small, between 20 to 40 centimeters in height. Again about 30 pieces would be made per day per person. Packed in bamboo baskets filled with straw, they would be shipped throughout the area of Mandalay.

Heads with elegance / Pottery after firing
優雅地將陶器頂在頭上運送 / 窯燒過後的陶壺

個人平均一天可以做三十件。成品裝在竹籃裡用稻草填滿後運送到曼德勒。

在村子裡閒逛的時候，我在路邊發現了一個裝滿小小陶製品籃子。我把稻草撥開來，看到一堆小小的動物，雞、馬、大象、兔子、貓、貓頭鷹，還有企鵝。這些小小的存錢筒正準備運往市場。這種具功能性的裝飾品其實有著傳統的客群，父母親會利用它們來教育小孩子存錢。我選了一組很漂亮的，我想要把它們介紹給仰光的市場。這行為的背後有我的原因。

在緬甸開放以前，這裡的生活好像停留在某個年代。鄉下地方用來維持經濟運作的方式已經好幾十年，甚至是好幾世紀、好幾千年都沒有改變過。製陶在最早的文明世界就有了，不只在緬甸，在世界各地都有。陶製品的發明一開始是為了實際的用途，之後才漸漸發展出藝術品的形式與樣貌，或是在實用的層面增添藝術氣息。不過對多數人來說，陶製品還是維持它最簡單的形式，讓一般的人都可以使用。

緬甸的製陶業，主要都是家庭工廠，或是整個村子一起從事製陶。如果未來就像商品交易一樣可被預期，那麼傳統的製陶業將會隨著時間以及緬甸的現代化而逐漸萎縮。一旦水管鋪好，自來水送進村子裡，人們就不太需要用陶壺

While browsing around the village, I suddenly saw one basket filled with smaller clay items sitting next to the village trail. When I picked through the straw, I saw tiny animals revealing themselves, chicken, horse, elephant, rabbit, cat, owl even a penguin. These are tiny piggy banks heading to the market. Such trinkets have their traditional customers, parents who want to teach children to save money. I chose a very beautiful set of animals and want to introduce such items to the market in Yangon. There is a reason behind my action.

Before Myanmar opens up a few years ago, life goes on as if in a time capsule. Rural community and its attached economy maintain itself the same for decades, centuries or even millennia. Pottery is as old as such early civilization, not only in Myanmar but throughout the world. They were created first for utilitarian use, and later developed into higher state for the select few as an art form, or utilitarian objects with artistic rendering. But it remains in its simplest form for usage by common people.

That is the case of Myanmar's pottery cottage industry, mainly home based and usually attached to entire village specializing in such preoccupation. If future is predictable like in commodity trading, traditional pottery will in time go into decline as the country of Myanmar modernizes. Once pipes are laid for running tap water into villages, people have little need to store water in these pottery containers. Furthermore, in the future plastic, metal and other

蓄水了。此外,塑膠,金屬跟其他耐用的容器,未來也將會取代這種易碎的陶製品。

目前這種陶製品的需求看起來很穩定,一成不變,好幾世代都是這樣。不過這種的主流產業或許會在沒有警訊之下,突然間消失。去保護這個夕陽家庭工業的其中一個方法是打進蓬勃的觀光市場,還有,讓當地的品味跟上國際上大城市的消費市場。為產品增加價值也是一種簡單的概念。如果這些小東西可以做得更細緻,像是上釉讓表面光滑,或是漸漸變成藝術品或雕塑品,那麼緬甸的製陶業在未來還是有市場的。

Pottery loading at village / 裝載陶器的舢舨

durable containers are also replacing breakable clay ones.

For now, the demand for such pottery utilitarian objects seems to be stable and at a constant, like it has for generations. However, something mainstream may without warning suddenly become obsolete. One way to safeguard this twilight of the cottage industry is to tap at the burgeoning tourist market as well as a more sophisticated local and international consumer market in big cities. Value-added to products also is a simple concept. If these small items can become more refined, like glazing to smooth the surface, or even gradually becoming an art or sculpture, there may just be a new future waiting for the pottery in Myanmar.

Animal treasure found / 可愛的各種陶製動物

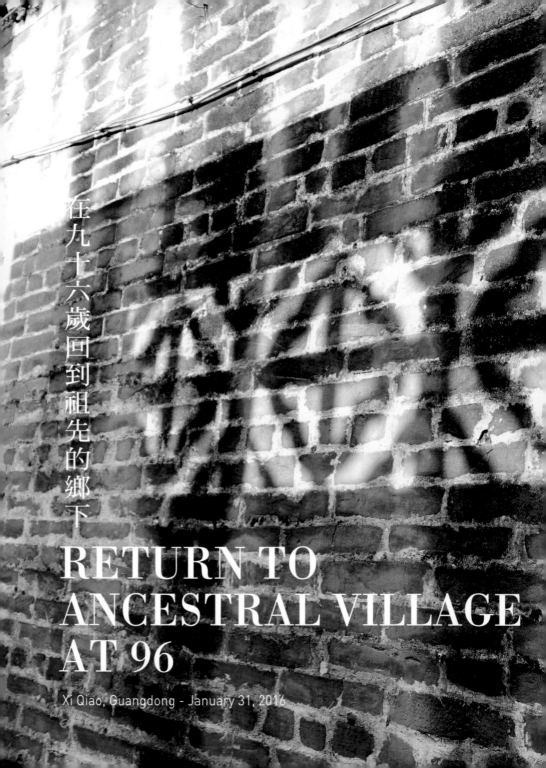

在九十六歲回到祖先的鄉下

RETURN TO ANCESTRAL VILLAGE AT 96

Xi Qiao, Guangdong - January 31, 2016

在九十六歲回到祖先的鄉下

我的父親出生於一九一九年的八月，今年已經九十六歲了。打從出生開始香港就是他的家。在將近一百年的時間裡，我父親拜訪過我們祖先的鄉下三次，最近的一趟，希望不會是最後的一趟，就是這兩天。

我的祖父黃錫祺 *Wong Sik Kee* 在年幼的時候離開南海縣的西樵村前往香港。南海位於廣州的西南方，距離廣州約七十公里，現在開車大約一個鐘頭。從香港開車要三個鐘頭，或者也可以在珠海港口搭船往來。總之從南海到香港這趟旅途對一個小男孩來說，好像是去到天邊那樣的遠。

祖父進入 *Queen's College*（皇仁書院），彌補他錯失接受教育的那幾年，三年內完成五年的高中學業。後來他從商，最終成為捷成洋行的買辦，那是一家丹麥與德國的貿易公司。他事業做得很成功所以被任命為買辦協會的理事長。

戰爭發生後，十個老婆跟三打小孩的負擔，讓家境變差。我的父親黃展華 *Wong Chin Wah* 是第七個兒子，必須中斷

RETURN TO ANCESTRAL VILLAGE AT 96

My father was born in August 1919 and is now well into his 96th year. Hong Kong has always been his home since birth. Over the span of almost a hundred years, my father has visited our ancestral village three times, latest, hopefully not last, being these two days.

My grandfather Wong Sik Kee left the village of Xi Qiao in Nanhai County for Hong Kong as a young boy. Nanhai is about 70 kilometers to the southwest of Guangzhou, roughly an hour's drive today. From Hong Kong it can be reached by car in three hours or by ferry to Pearl River ports nearby. However from Nanhai to Hong Kong a century ago was like reaching the end of the sky for a boy.

My grandfather entered Queen's College and made up his lost years in education, completing five years of high school within three years, skipping every other year. He later entered business, ultimately becoming the Comprador of the Jebsen Company, the Danish/German trading house. He was successful enough to be nominated as Chairman of the Comprador Association.

在香港大學醫學院的學業，以難民的身分進入中國。在戰爭的時期，他設法在桂林完成化學的學業。戰後他回到香港，一輩子都在九龍的天主教華仁中學當科學教師。

我們搭了兩小時的船回到西樵。當地政府接待我們的方式有點太隆重。畢竟不太常有這樣年紀的人返鄉。入住豪華的西樵飯店後我們被帶到祿舟，祖先的村莊。我的祖父曾經是個很成功的生意人，但是財富不在時，影響力也不在。不像藝術家，不管他們是富有還是貧窮，名聲還是存在。

祿舟村出的藝術家不管是美術還是武術，在華人世界都很

Red and Gray brick house / 紅灰磚房子

War came and the burden of ten wives and three dozen children took its toll and the family went into decline. My father Wong Chin Wah who came seventh among the sons had to cut short his Medical School education at Hong Kong University and left for China as a refugee. He managed to finish his studies in Chemistry during war-time in Guilin. After the War, he became a life-long educator in Science at the Jesuit Wah Yan College in Kowloon.

Our return to Xi Qiao was by a two-hour boat ride. The reception by the local government was a bit ceremonious. After all, it is unusual for someone of such advanced age to return home. After checking into the posh Xi Qiao Hotel, we were whisked off to Luzhou, my ancestor's home village. My grandfather,

Locked doors / 上鎖的門

出名，甚至在世界上。黃君璧在華人世界就很出名。他以山水畫著名。連蔣介石的夫人都曾是他的學生。一九四九年黃君璧移居到台灣，與其他兩位國畫大師張大千，溥心畬齊名。

比其他藝術家都還要出名的應該是武術家黃飛鴻。幾乎每個華人都知道他，聽到他的名就好像聽到鼓聲跟功夫電影的配樂，關於他的電影超過百部，許多出自於五零到六零年代的黑白片。現代寬螢幕彩色版的在國際上也很受到歡迎。設在黃飛鴻紀念館的醒獅團也常得獎，二零一五年的國際比賽裡贏得好幾座金牌。

我們祖先老家出的人才比村莊有名，但是西樵還是有其他可以引以為傲的地方。西樵山名列廣東省最美麗的四座山之一。西樵大餅也有五百年的歷史，比其他地方的中國人，這裡的人更早知道糕餅這東西。白色大餅上面撒著糖粉，有些直徑達十二吋。另一項村裡出名的手工藝品，就是最適合農夫夏天戴的大頂的手編竹帽了。

欣賞舞獅後，父親特別受邀去領取一個象徵性的紅袋子，袋子上面用綠色的萵苣裝飾，被掛在很危險的位置，是為獅子採青，而那裝飾美麗的獅子很輕巧地就將它取下來。紀念館跟舞獅表演地點緊鄰我們的村莊，走幾步路就轉進巷子裡。幾乎所有的房子，包括一些很精緻的，

being a successful businessman of the past, held little weight once the fortune was gone. Unlike artists, their fame tend to stay, be they rich or poor.

And at Luzhou village, both type of artists, fine art and martial art, are renowned throughout the Chinese world, perhaps even internationally. Wong Junbi represents the former. He was a traditional Chinese artist most famous for his landscape paintings. Even Madame Chiang Kai-shek became his student. Wong left for Taiwan in 1949 and became one of three most famous painters there, the others being Zhang Daqin and Fu Xinyu.

Perhaps more famous than the fine artist is martial artist Wong Fei-hung. With almost everyone in a Chinese household young and old, his name rings with the drums and Kung Fu music from over a hundred films, most of them in black & white early flicks of the 1950s and 60s. More modern versions also became an international hits with wide screen and full color. The Lion Dance Troupe, based at the Wong Fei Hung memorial hall, has won numerous awards, including several Gold trophies during the international competition in 2015.

Thus our ancestral home is better known more by its sons rather than by name of the village. Xi Qiao however has other claims to fame and glory. Xi Qiao Shan is one of the four most beautiful mountains of Guangdong Province. The Xi Qiao big cake has a history of over 500 years, long before baked cakes are

用堅固的「淺綠色」磚塊蓋的房子現在都失修了，也都
沒有人住。村民們大多都搬到附近新的華廈。即使如此，
中國新年將近，每棟房子的門口都貼上春聯，連失修的
房子也有貼。

很快地話傳開來，一位近百歲的老人回來了。一些知道我
祖父的長輩們開始走出來。不到一會兒，一位年輕的遠房
親戚出現。在他的幫助下，他帶我們到我祖父曾經擁有房
子的其中一間。當地人說的方言我跟父親都聽不懂，我覺
得有點尷尬。不過黃家人還是非常的好客，他們很好意地
要留我們下來吃頓飯還是炸些特別的點心給我們吃，但是
我們婉拒了。

known to China. White in color with a sprinkle of powder sugar splashed on it, some can measure up to over twelve inches in diameter. The handweaved huge bamboo hats, ideal for use by farmers in the field, is another novelty and handicraft of the village.

After observing the Lion Dancer performance, my father was specially invited to receive a symbolic red packet with green lettuce which the decorated lion retrieved from a most precarious suspended position. The Memorial Hall and Lion Dancer performance is directly adjacent to our village. A short walk took us inside the village alleys. Almost all houses, some extremely refined and built with hard "pale green" bricks but now in disrepair, are vacant. Villagers have mostly moved into nearby multi-storied new houses. Nonetheless, as Chinese New Year is just around the corner, house-gracing door poems are pasted on almost every old house, even dilapidated ones.

Soon, words got around that a senior, more or less a centenarian, has returned home. Some older folks who had heard of my grandfather's name began converging. Before long, a distant but young relative showed up. With his help, we were directed to one of the many houses my grandfather used to own. The local dialect is unintelligible to both my father and to me, which made me feel a little awkward. But the Wong's are nonetheless extremely hospitable. We declined their offer to serve us a meal or the frying of some special dessert.

My father receiving honor / 作者父親接受表彰

隔天早上霧氣瀰漫，我們到山上去走走，真是愉快。在「方竹」花園的時候，我問保全有沒有可能可以讓我買一些方竹帶回香港種。「沒有用，有人試過，試到罵髒話。這竹子一旦種在別的地方長出來就是圓的，不會是方的！」他回答說。然而跟以往一樣，我從不接受「不」這個答案。

在花園的大門我跟阿凡聊起來，阿凡在天后宮的廟前賣香。「沒問題！三百塊，賣給你幾株方竹，含莖跟土。我們的竹子就連肉眼看起來都很方正，不只是摸起來的感覺而已……」她自誇的說，「還有，我們的村子 *Wan Dyun* 離這裡很近。」她重申。我說：「那裏是我好友祖先的村莊，我的朋友是馬萬祺的孫子。」「是的，整個村莊都是姓馬，馬萬祺也捐了五十萬給村裡的寺廟修繕」阿凡說。

隨後我們的車子跟著她的摩托車在雨中上山去。在山腰的地方經過一些魚塘，最後抵達馬家的村子。阿凡已經事先連絡好了，一位中年男子在屋後正在挖年輕的竹子給我。十五分鐘後我們往山下走，前往下一站釣魚用品店。

「這個東西在香港價錢是兩到三倍，你最好在這裡買。」用品店的老闆說。「你有賣竹子做的魚竿嗎？」我問道。「別開玩笑了，現在沒有人用那個了」他回答。而這正是我最希望聽到的了。「請你給我這個裝魚竿的長袋子，我

Our visit up the mountain in misty weather the next morning was also a delightful experience. While visiting a "Square Bamboo" Garden, I asked the security guard whether it was possible to buy some for relocation to my Hong Kong garden. "No use, people have tried and ended up cursing and swearing. Once planted elsewhere, they came out round instead of square," he answered. As always, I won't take "no" as answer.

At the gate of the garden, I chatted with Afang, the lady selling joss sticks in front of the Tianhou Goddess Temple. "Surely for three hundred dollars, we can sell you a few square bamboo, even with roots and soil attached. Our bamboo even looks square, not just square to the feel of the hand," she boasted. "Our village is Wan Dyun, a short distance from here," she reiterated. "But that's where my good friend, grandson of Ma Wanqi, has their ancestral village," I added. "Indeed, the entire village are Ma's and Ma Wanqi donated half a million for the ancestral temple repair," Afang said.

Before long, our cars were following her motor scooter up the hill in misty rain. Passing some fish ponds at mid mountain, we ended at the Ma's village. Afang had called ahead and a middle age man was busy behind the house digging up a few young bamboos for me. Within fifteen minutes, I was on my way down the mountain with my next stop a fishing equipment store.

"Prices in Hong Kong are twice to three times higher. You better buy it here,"

已經有竹子了。我還要摺疊式的漁網。還有那牆上顏色鮮
豔的救生背心。」我邊說邊趕緊把我買的東西裝到袋子裡。

一手抓著父親的手臂，另一邊的肩上背著裝有所有釣魚工
具的包包，我在想，如果被海關攔下來的話，我可是有故
事可說的。既然現在沒有人賣竹子做的魚竿，那麼我要把
這些竹子帶回香港種，再用種出來的竹子做魚竿給父親。
當然海關不需要知道這是來自我祖先村莊的竹子，以及它
們有多麼非常珍貴。而且它們不是圓的，是方的！

quipped the fishing store owner. "Do you sell bamboo fishing rod?" I asked. "No one use those anymore, are you kidding?" came the answer. That's exactly what I hope to hear. "Please give me this long container bag for the rod, I already have the bamboo. I'll take this collapsible fishing net as well. And up there on the wall, that colorful life vest," I rushed to bag my purchases.

With all my fishing gear in a bag over my shoulder and holding my aging father by the arm, I expect if the customs officer were to stop me, I have my story spelled out. Since no bamboo fishing rods are available, I am taking these bamboos home to Hong Kong to grow them into my father's fishing rods. Of course, they don't need to know that these bamboos from my home village are special and highly valued. They came not round, but square!

Father & son at square bamboo grove / 作者和父親合影於四方竹園前

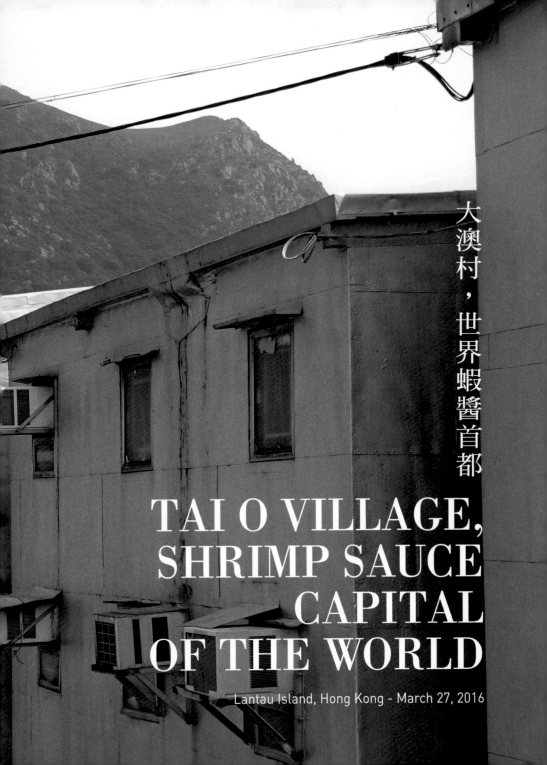

大澳村，世界蝦醬首都

TAI O VILLAGE, SHRIMP SAUCE CAPITAL OF THE WORLD

Lantau Island, Hong Kong - March 27, 2016

大澳村，世界蝦醬首都

「看看這塊紅樹林，種它們的人真的很不負責任！」鄭啟強不悅地說。關於大澳村的事，鄭先生很勇於發聲，曾經是大嶼山原始的漁村，直到新機場（一九九八年完工）跟迪士尼樂園（二零零五）完工前，這裡一直是個落後的小島。一直到一九七零年代，這裡都還是個被孤立的村子，而今天大批大批的觀光客在周末來到大澳村，參觀像迷宮般的鐵皮屋跟商店。

「只要這一點就可以陳述重點，我認為從城市來的人覺得他們受過比較高的教育，需要為這裡做些改變。這類象徵性的動作，都以保育之名讓他們拿到政府或是民間的補助。」鄭先生不屑的說：「你看到那些在水裡的垃圾跟保麗龍箱子，全部都卡在樹下，他們也從來不清。很不切實際，而且狀況比以前還糟！」他指向一整排沿著走道一直到他店鋪新種下的紅樹林。

我可以理解也同情他的無奈。我看過類似的狀況，所謂的「保育人士」渲染將瀕危的棲息地和物種，這跟金融界的

TAI O VILLAGE,
SHRIMP SAUCE CAPITAL OF THE WORLD

"Look at this patch of mangrove, I feel the people planting them are totally irresponsible," said Cheng Kai-keung with disgust in his face. Cheng is very vocal about many things in and around Tai O, once a backwater fishing village of Lantau, itself an island backwater of Hong Kong, that is until the new airport and Disneyland were completed in 1998 and 2005 respectively. An isolated village up until the 1970s, today droves of tourists come to Tai O during the weekends to visit a labyrinth of metal shed houses and shops.

"Just a tiny patch to make a point. I think city folks coming here feel they are educated and needed to make change. Such symbolic action help them receive government or private resources, all in the name of conservation," Cheng added with a sneer in his tone. "See all the trash and foam boxes in the water caught under the trees, they never follow up and clean up the mess. It is impractical and worse than before," Cheng spoke while pointing at a line of mangroves along the footpath to his shop.

I can understand and sympathize with his frustration. After all, I have seen

Sunning to make salt fish / 晾曬鹹魚干

similar situations acted out by "conservationists", taking endangered habitats and species on a spin, not unlike spin artists of our financial world. At times it becomes a branding exercise, hijacking public sentiments for fundraising or recognition needs. But of course, there are also committed conservationists with more purist agendas, though not always acted out with sensitivity or consideration for other stakeholders.

When it comes to his own family business, Cheng became more meticulous and solemn. "Cheng Cheung Hing, our brand, was founded four generations ago in 1920 by my great grandfather," Cheng said proudly. "It is a real tradition. We specialize in making the finest shrimp sauce and shrimp paste, known throughout the world where ever there are sizable Chinese communities," said Cheng. "In fact, we sell more to overseas Chinese than locally," Cheng said emphatically.

"Eating at home together is a very important tradition among overseas Chinese, thus their habits, flavor and taste is carried from one generation to the next," he explained. "With our shrimp sauce and paste, Cantonese in particular

騙子有什麼不同。有的時候這是品牌操作的伎倆，綁架大眾的情緒，為了募款或是獲得認同。當然也有認真的保育人士，出發點是純真的，雖然有時候不夠細膩，欠缺思考未把利益相關者考慮進去。

說到鄭先生的家族事業時，他變得很嚴肅也細密。「鄭祥興，是我們的品牌，是我曾祖父在一九二零年創立的。」鄭先生驕傲的說：「這真的是傳統，我們專門製作最好的蝦醬跟蝦膏，世界各地有華人的地方都知道我們！事實上我們賣去國外給海外華人的數量比本地的還多。」他強調。

「對海外的華人來說，在家一起吃飯是很重要的，習慣、風味、口味才能傳承下去。」他解釋。「用我們的蝦醬跟蝦膏最可以讓人跟過去連結，尤其是廣東人！」他告訴我們為什麼他家的品牌沒有隨著時間消失，反而經營的很好。

「猜猜看誰是我們最忠誠的顧客？」他問。我回答的兩個答案台山跟汕頭都不對。「在北美的越南華人是我們最大的客戶，他們可是吃上癮了！」他微笑著說。

即使對一個成功的老牌子來說，日子也不是一直都這麼輕鬆的。二零一三年開始香港政府禁止近海捕撈，做

Cheng Kai-keung and mother / 鄭啟強和母親

feel connected to their past, the ancestral home in China where they came from," Cheng told us his theory of why their brand continued to catch on and did not die with time.

"Guess who are our most loyal customers," Cheng asked. I suggested two answers - Taishan and Swatow Chinese - both wrong. "Vietnamese Chinese in North America are by far our biggest customers; to them it is like an

蝦醬蝦膏主要的原料「銀蝦」已經被過度捕撈。鄭先生只好轉向中國尋找蝦仔貨源。做蝦膏的程序很多道，不需要新鮮的蝦仔。但是做蝦醬就需要用新鮮的蝦仔去發酵。設定好供應鏈變得很重要，因為蝦仔必須要準時送到。到今天，鄭先生每年出產三十到四十噸的蝦醬跟蝦膏；而以前，他可以做到一百噸。

用來醃漬蝦仔的海鹽以前是用當地產的，大澳村有長久的產鹽歷史。但是在一九七零年代初期這行業就幾乎停擺，所以現在鄭先生用的鹽都是從外地來的。製鹽業就跟農業，養豬業一樣，就像在太陽底下都被蒸發掉了。當最後的幾隻豬正被吃掉的時候，水牛則被放生。到今天還看得到水牛在大嶼山漫遊。

現在大澳村只剩下兩家蝦醬店，幾十年前還有十家。蝦醬聞起來的味道很嗆，這風味不是所有人都可以接受的。空氣中充滿了這味道，離鄭先生的店二、三十公尺都還聞得到。他的母親負責店頭的零售，店的後面則是用來包裝跟送貨。一箱二十四罐，棧板上的箱子再用繩子固定，然後用堆高機運送到城裡，將貨品送到世界各地的批發商。有些貨品會出現在北美的市場，其他則是運到歐洲。

高高的儲藏閣樓上有些木盆，像在歐洲用來做葡萄酒那種。鄭先生把這些容器當成文物，因為現在用的工具已經

addiction," Cheng revealed with a smile.

But life isn't always a party, even with an old and successful brand. Since Hong Kong government implemented restrictions on near-shore fishing in 2013, the supply of "silver shrimp", the key ingredient of the sauce and paste, became exhausted. Cheng had to turn to China for supply of his shrimp. Making the paste is a long process and doesn't require fresh shrimp. But making the sauce must be based on fermentation of freshly caught shrimp. Setting up his supply chain became crucial, so as to receive his shrimp in a timely fashion. Today Cheng produces between 30 to 40 tons of shrimp sauce and paste each year. In the past, he could deliver up to 100 tons.

Sea salt used in preserving these shrimp used to be produced locally, as Tai O had a long history of harvesting salt from the sea. Since the early 1970s, however, that profession had come to an end here, and today Cheng's salt is brought in from outside. Salt production, like farming and raising pigs, evaporated under the sun into obscurity. While the last pigs were eaten, the water buffaloes were simply let loose. They roam throughout Lantau Island to this day.

Today Tai O has only two shrimp sauce shops remaining, down from ten shops a few decades ago. The smell is pungent, but it is a fragrant aroma to those with the acquired taste. It fills the air within twenty or thirty meters of

現代化，變成很大的塑膠容器。當問到工具換了，味道是不是還一樣，鄭先生靜靜地將視線移開，沒有回答。

告訴我們歷史跟產品的製造過程後，鄭先生帶我們去他的祖厝，就在店鋪對面。這是我們來這裡的主要原因，檢視這間殘破的房子。Yutaka 是我們建築保存的專家朋友，他對這部分最感興趣，也開始拍照做紀錄。從台灣來的民族學家余舜德教授則是好奇村民住在這樣緊密的家庭結構裡，他們怎麼生活。

我，則是在考慮是否將這棟屋子放進 CERS 修復的項目

Shrimp paste and oyster / Drying of shrimp sauce · 蝦膏與蠔干 / 曬蝦醬

Cheng's shop. His mother takes care of the shop-front retail business, whereas in the back are the packaging and delivery departments. Bottles are put into carton boxes of 24 bottles each, string bundled into crates, then taken into town with a forklift, and sent off to wholesalers worldwide. Some of these bottles would show up in markets in North America. Others are destined for Europe.

High up on a storage loft are old wooden basins, not unlike those used in grape wine making in Europe. Cheng kept these containers simply as relics, as today's utensils have been modernized into large plastic vessels. When asked whether the product tastes the same with the change of processing equipment,

中。到二樓起居室的木頭樓梯已經變得很脆弱，很危險，一次只能上去一個人。祖先的神壇還在，乾淨整齊，就在瓦片屋頂下的小閣樓上。很明顯的鄭先生跟家人還是持續燒香，儘管屋況已經不能住人了。這種尊敬祖先的傳統最令人欽佩。

假如我們真的有能力可以再添加一個修復的項目，也許我要開始學著習慣蝦醬的氣味，但是我不吃。或許假以時日我會覺得它很香，雖然味道很重。那是未來的事。今天我就帶一罐回家當作紀念，封的好好的一罐。

Cheng quietly looked away and did not answer.

After revealing the history and process of making these products, Cheng proceeded to show us the ancestral house across from his shop. This is one of the main reasons for our visit, to inspect a dilapidated house. Yutaka, our conservation architect friend, is most interested in this part of the visit and begins making photographic records. Professor Yu Shuenn-der, an ethnologist from Taiwan, is also curious as to how villagers lived in the past within a close family structure.

I, on the other hand, am contemplating whether this might become a CERS project in restoration. The wooden stairs to the second floor living area has become so fragile and dangerous that only one person can go up at a time. The ancestral altar still stands clean and tidy, presiding over a small loft under the tiled roof. Obviously Cheng and his family have been keeping the incense burning despite the house itself being no longer livable. That tradition of respect to ancestors is most admirable.

If indeed we have the capacity to take on yet another conservation project, perhaps I have to start learning how to breathe shrimp sauce odor, even if I am not going to eat it. Perhaps in time I too would find it a fragrant aroma, rather than a pungent smell. That however is for the future. Today, I am taking home just one bottle as souvenir, sealed well.

現在的一百歲其實是新八十歲？

IS ONE HUNDRED
THE NEW EIGHTY?

Dateline Pacific – April 7/8, 2016

現在的一百歲其實是新八十歲？

「使用手冊上面說這部機器適合八十五歲以下使用！」陳文寬笑著說。他指的是剛剛在他腳下的 *NordicTrack* 跑步機。「我下週就要一百零二歲了⋯⋯」他小聲說，好像在說祕密。

認識他的人或是聽過他的人都知道他的年紀。他大多數的朋友都已經逝去了，倒是聽過他的人還很多。陳文寬是位有名的飛行員，二十世紀的中國飛行員。

他不僅創立兩家航空公司，也載過許多政要，像蔣介石，杜立德將軍。在那動盪不安的時代，亞洲區有好幾場戰爭和衝突，他曾出過不少危險又機密的任務，包括空拋、撤退，和營救。飛越駝峰跟開闢新路線，或是從新疆跨過喜瑪拉雅西部進入巴基斯坦，這只是他眾多豐功偉業的其中兩項。

其他的人在他這年紀已經慢下腳步，以蝸牛般的速度，開始倒數剩下的日子。但這不是陳文寬，他才剛把他的

IS ONE HUNDRED THE NEW EIGHTY?

"The instruction manual said this machine is for use by those under the age of 85," Moon Chin said with a small grin on his face. He was referring to his NordicTrack that he just stepped off from. "And I am turning 102 next week," he whispered as if letting out a secret.

But his age is no secret to anyone who knows him, or knows of him. Indeed, almost all of his acquaintances have passed away, but of those who knew of him, there are plenty. Moon is one of the best known aviators, Chinese aviators, of the 20th Century.

Not only did he co-found two airline companies, he flew many dignitaries, like Chiang Kai-shek and General Doolittle, and took on many dangerous and secret missions, including airdrops, evacuations and rescues, during the turbulent and heady days of the past, spanning several wars and conflicts in Asia. Flying the Hump and pioneering a new flight path across the western Himalayas from Xinjiang into Pakistan were just two of his many accomplishments.

新玩具拆封。「特價兩千九百九十九元！」他說。「所以我把跑步機換成這台，設定為每次運動五分鐘。」他說的很輕鬆。

舊的跑步機用的是電動馬達，而新的這台 NordicTrack 用的是使用者的體力跟力量。每一步都需要腿，手，身體實在的出力，在他的年紀其實需要的是更多的意志力。「不用五分鐘，就像在爬五層樓的樓梯，每層樓等於有二十階梯，不間斷。」他跟我解釋他的計算。

不過，這運動的重點在於不間斷，就像陳文寬怎麼面對他的生命。我讀到在他面前 LCD 螢幕上的倒數數字：0:15，0:14，0:13......當秒數漸漸減少，他的腳步開始加快，好像短跑者衝刺終點一樣。這位百歲老人即使在這年紀腳步依舊沒有慢下來。陳文寬還是充滿活力，他的生命充滿回憶。我開玩笑說他的運動是「月球漫步」（因為他的英文名字是 Moon），可與阿波羅號的阿姆斯壯踏上月球的第一步相比。

兩個月前陳文寬打電話告訴我醫生不准他出遠門，因此我們取消了原本要帶他回廣東台山的老家的行程，他在一九二四年離開，那年他才十歲。

醫生的命令並沒有讓他慢下腳步，至少在跑步機上沒有，

Others his age may have slowed down to a snail's pace, counting their remaining and waning days. Not so for Moon, who has just unpacked his new toy machine. "It was on sale for two thousand nine hundred and ninety nine dollars," he said. "So I replaced my treadmill for this, and set it for five minutes each time I use it," Moon added as a simple matter of fact.

The treadmill was run by an electric motor, whereas this NordicTrack is operated using your own energy and power. Each step, followed by the next, requires a real effort of legs, hands and body, which at Moon's age requires more of his strong mind. "Within five minutes, it is like climbing five stories of stairs, each floor being equivalent to about twenty steps, non-stop," Moon explained to me the metrics of his exercise.

However, the emphasis to this exercise is the non-stop part, just like how Moon has dealt with his life. I could read the count-down on the LCD screen displayed in front of him. 0:15, 0:14, 0:13. As the seconds dropped, I could see his steps quicken, like a sprinter on his home stretch to the finish line. This is no centenarian stepping down from a pedestal with eclipsing year. Moon is still full of life, and full of memories. I jokingly referred to his exercise as 'Moon step,' in comparison to that of Apollo mission astronaut Armstrong's first step on the Moon.

Only two months ago, Moon informed me over the phone that his doctor was restricting his long distance travel. Thus we had to cancel a trip for him to

到現在每餐都還會喝個一瓶啤酒。就在一天前我們一起去了卡梅爾海，兩天一夜的行程，去看稀有的骨董車收藏，是一位友人費盡心思收集來的。陳文寬在八十幾歲的時候買了最後一部瑪莎拉蒂，兩年前他訂購最新一款的賓士 *AGM c63*，但是他在一百歲的時候卻沒有辦法更新他的駕照。這台非常棒的車現在放在他的車庫裡，我偶爾來的時候會把它開出來。

如果你覺得這位百歲老人是個異數，那你可要看看前幾天跟我在紐約一起午飯的這位先生。我站在中央車站時鐘亭的旁邊，「不好意思我遲了五分鐘！」一個沉穩的聲音從我背後傳來。我轉身看到 *Peter Goutiere*，我這一百零二歲的飛行員朋友，他穿著優雅的風衣戴著毛帽。很快地我們在有名的 *Oyster Bar* 找到我們習慣坐的位置。他啜飲著馬丁尼，點了他常叫的蛤蠣濃湯還有龍蝦卷。「要確定是白色的那種喔！」*Peter* 提醒服務生他點的是新英格蘭濃湯而不是曼哈頓版的。

「那些日子，我經常順道去旁邊的泛美（*PanAm*）大樓，今天已成為 *MetLife* 大樓。」*Peter* 提醒我他的記憶還是完好的。他一九一四年在印度出生，爸爸是法國人媽媽是英國人，一九二八年他十四歲的時候去了美國。一九四零年他拿到機師執照，太平洋戰爭開打時他在西非加入泛美航空（*Pan American*），之後被調到中國，當中國航空公

return to his home village of Taishan in Guangdong, a place he left when he was ten years old, in 1924.

The doctor's orders, however, did not slow him down, at least not on his exercise machine, or when he downed a whole glass of beer with every meal. Just a day ago, we went on an overnight trip to Carmel by the Sea, to view a rare collection of antique cars a friend had meticulously assembled. When Moon was into his eighties, he bought his last Maserati, and just two years ago ordered his latest model Mercedes AGM c63, though he did not manage to renew his driving license at age 100. Today this very fine car is kept in his garage, pulling out only when I occasionally stopped by to visit him.

But if you should feel Moon is an exception for a centenarian, what about someone I just had lunch with a few days ago in New York? I was standing beside the center clock kiosk at noon at Grand Central. "Sorry I am five minutes late," came a solid and reassuring voice from behind me. I turned around, and there it was in front of me Peter Goutiere, my other 102-year-old pilot friend, in an elegant beige trench coat and a wool hat. Soon we found our usual seat near the corner of the famous Oyster Bar. Sipping his martini, Peter ordered his usual clam chowder and a lobster roll. "Make sure it is the white kind," Pete told the waiter to make sure they serve his favorite New England rather than the Manhattan version of the soup.

司的飛行員。戰爭那幾年他出過六百八十趟駝峰的飛行任務。他當年的航空日誌跟飛行計算機現在都放在 CERS 石澳的展示館。

後來他成為聯邦航空署（FAA）的檢定機長。在一九七零年他是最早一批全新波音 747 大型噴射機的飛行員，同時也負責檢定哪些飛行員可以飛這款大飛機。他一直在聯邦航空署工作到一九九零年退休。陳文寬在一百歲的時候買了一台全新的賓士，兩年前當 Peter 即將一百歲的那個月，他把 DC-3 飛上天空，坐的是左邊的機長座位。這 DC-3 跟 CNAC 第 100 號就是同一款的飛機，在一九四五年的時候他從美國交付這架全新的飛機到中國。

我們分手前他特別用他小時候學的印度話跟我說話，那讓我非常開心。「你知道在戰爭的時候，有一次在加爾各答，我用印度話跟一個服務生說話，這讓我的副駕駛好驚訝……」Peter 再次跟我說起這個他最喜歡的故事。「當他問我怎麼會說他們的語言時，我回他，喂！我已經來這裡十天了！」。「他不知道我是在印度出生的！」Peter 用他一貫的幽默說著。

我最近也很開心，享受跟這些百歲的「老」友在一起的時光。就在兩週前，我跟機長楊積（Jack Young）在香港吃午餐，他那天晚點要回到他在加拿大蒙特婁的家。Jack

"In those days, I often stopped by the PanAm Building next door. Today it is the MetLife Building," Peter reminded me that his memory is still intact. Born in India in 1914 to a French father and English mother, Pete came to America as a teenager in 1928. He acquired his pilot license in 1940. When the War broke out in the Pacific, he joined Pan America in West Africa, and later was transferred to China, flying for CNAC. During the remaining years of the War, Peter flew over 680 missions over the Hump. Today his log book and flight computer from that era are on display at the CERS Shek O Exhibit House.

Later Peter was to become a Check Pilot for the Federal Aviation Agency (FAA). He was one of the first to be certified for flying the new Boeing 747 Jumbo planes in 1970, as well as checking-out other pilots to qualify to fly the huge machine. He continued working for the FAA until retiring in 1990. While Moon bought his new Mercedes at age 100, Pete trumped that by taking to the air in a DC-3 the month of his 100th birthday two years ago, in the cockpit on the left seat as Captain. That was exactly the same airplane, CNAC Ship 100, that he delivered brand new from the U.S. to China in 1945.

Before we parted, Pete regaled me by speaking in his childhood tongue of Hindi. "You know one time in Calcutta during the War, my co-pilot was totally shocked that I was speaking Hindi to a service boy," Pete retold one of his favorite stories. "When he asked me how come I spoke their language. I answered, 'Hell? I've been here for ten days already!'" "He didn't know that I

在尖沙咀的飯店現身，他總是穿的很講究，頭戴紳士帽，脖子圍著絲巾，穿著他最喜歡的藍色麂皮夾克，很像飛行夾克。

Jack 一九一四年在舊金山出生。考取飛行執照後在一九三零年代的中期加入廣東空軍，在那時候是由軍閥陳濟棠帶領。一九三六年他飛到南京時整個空軍都倒戈投向國民黨。戰爭期間他一開始在中國航空公司擔任陳文寬的副駕駛，然後漸漸成為客機跟貨機的正駕駛。

戰爭結束後 Jack 加入陳文寬成立的中央航空運輸公司（CATC）。一九四九年十一月，十二架飛機叛逃（大陸方稱之為「起義」）到新成立的中華人民共和國，Jack 是其中一架的駕駛。後來他回到香港在香港飛機工程有限公司工作，擔任飛機維修部門的主管，一直到他退休為止。

「你知道不知道是什麼原因我的身分證上的生日顯示我是一九一七年生的，這讓我可以多工作個三年才退休。」Jack 安靜地跟我透露。他通常都很安靜好像深陷在他的思緒與回憶裡，我們相識久了他終於放心將他的秘密告訴我。到現在 Jack 每年依舊會搭乘橫跨太平洋的飛機兩次。

當帳單來的時候，Jack 非常堅持要付錢，他說因為他比我年長。我同意，因為我都叫他 Jack Old，而不是 Jack

Checking satellite image of Shanghai / 觀看上海衛星影像

was born in India," Pete spoke with his usual wit and humor.

Lately I tend to regale as well, enjoying myself by staying around these centenarian friends of mine. Just two weeks ago while in Hong Kong, I went out to a buffet lunch with Captain Jack Young, right before he was to board a flight back to his Canadian home in Montreal. Always dressed meticulously with a gentleman's cap over his head and a silk scarf around his neck, Jack appeared at a hotel in Tsim Sha Tsui in his favorite blue suede jacket, similar to a flight jacket.

Jack was born in San Francisco in 1914. After securing his flight license, he joined the Guangdong Air Force in the mid-1930s. At the time, it was under the rule of a Warlord Chan Ji-tong. He flew to Nanjing in 1936 when the entire Air Force defected to join the Nationalists. During the War he flew for CNAC and started as a co-pilot for Moon Chin before being checked out as a full captain on both passenger and cargo planes.

Young。我每次這樣叫他，他都笑的好開心。內心裡他永遠都是 *Jack Young*。

CERS 正在製作一個紀錄片，向這三位超過百歲的飛行員致敬。我希望九月的時候將片子帶到舊金山做首映，屆時陳文寬，*Peter* 跟 *Jack* 也會一起參加，這僅存的，曾在戰爭時擔任中國航空公司的飛行員也可以重聚。對我而言，我也快七十歲了，遇見這些百歲朋友讓我覺得我好像是個年輕人。這給我動力，邁向光明的未來，並持續我個人探險旅途的挑戰。真的，別試圖說服我，現在的一百歲其實不過是新的八十歲！

At Oyster Bar / 作者與「老」友共聚 Oyster Bar

After the War, Jack joined Central Air Transport Corp (CATC) that Moon had started. In November 1949, Jack piloted one of the twelve airplanes that defected to the newly founded People's Republic. Later he was to return to Hong Kong and worked for Haeco as head of aircraft maintenance until his retirement.

"You know, for some reason my I.D. card has me down as being born in 1917 and that allowed me to work three extra years before having to retire," Jack confided to me quietly. Usually very quiet as if into his own thoughts and memories, our gradual acquaintance finally gave Jack confidence to reveal some secrets of his era. Today, Jack still jets across the Pacific twice a year.

As the bill came, Jack was adamant that he was older than me and must pay for the meal. I concurred as I called him by the name I gave him, Jack Old, rather than Jack Young. A big smile would come to his face every time I called him by that name. But in spirit he would always be Jack Young.

CERS is finishing a documentary film celebrating life past one hundred featuring these three centenarian pilot friends. I hope to bring it to San Francisco in September for its premiere showing, when Moon, Peter and Jack will all be on hand for a reunion of the three remaining pilots of CNAC during the War. For myself, fast approaching 70, meeting these centenarian friends makes me feel like a young man. It also offers impetus for me to look forward to a promising future, a challenge for me to continue with my own journey of exploration. Indeed, no one should try convincing me that 100 is not the new 80!

菲律賓的懸棺

HANGING COFFINS OF THE PHILIPPINES

Sagada, Philippines – April 25, 2016

菲律賓的懸棺

也許聽起來有點奇怪，我正在寫有關懸棺的文章，而此刻我眼前的懸棺的所在地，就在我住的民宿下方不遠處。從我的書桌到懸棺的位置大概只有兩百到三百公尺，書桌前的空中花園懸掛在峽谷上，底下的河水會隨季節變得湍急。四個木棺靠著已經發白的碎片懸掛在石灰石的峭壁。

我的新朋友「Nash」是個作家，也是我們的「嚮導」，她選了這家民宿，但是不知道這麼剛好它就正對著懸棺，這是我們這趟來的主要原因。這間房子的顏色是水蜜桃色，從足球場走到這裡只要五分鐘，但非常隱密，跟懸棺一樣。就連熟悉這區域的加拿大人類學家 Joachim Voss 都不知道這裡。他在一九七六年第一次來到這裡研究薩加達的伊哥洛特人，這主題後來成為他的博士論文。

自此之後 Joachim 跟他的妻子 Villia，她也是位人類學家，每年都會來這裡好幾次，跟當地人住在一起，他們漸漸愛上這裡的人。很明顯的當地人也很喜歡他們。Joachim 帶

HANGING COFFINS OF THE PHILIPPINES

It seems strange that I should be writing about the Hanging Coffins while looking at one such coffin site slightly below the Bed and Breakfast where I am staying. From my desk, which overhangs a garden that drops off to a gorge with a seasonally surging river, the coffin site may only be two to three hundred meters across from me. Four wooden coffins hang against a whitish patch on the limestone cliff.

When Nash, my new writer friend and "guide", picked this B&B, she had no idea that it directly faced a site with hanging coffins, the chief purpose of my visit. The house, peach in color and five-minutes walk down from a football field, is well hidden, just like the nearby coffins. Even Canadian anthropologist Joachim Voss, who knew this area well, did not know of its existence. Since his first visit in 1976, Joachim had been studying the Igorot people of Sagada, which later became the focus of his doctoral thesis.

Since then, Joachim and his wife Villia, also an anthropologist, have been coming back several times a year to live among these people that they have learned to love. Obviously the feeling is reciprocal. As Joachim showed me

Coffin group / 懸棺群

around the region, passers-by waved or nodded at him.

Just yesterday afternoon, soon after I arrived at Sagada, Joachim took me on a hike into Echo Valley, a gorge where the most popular coffin site is. From a small path next to the Episcopal Church, we took a short cut to join the main trail toward the coffin site. Suddenly, it seemed I had rejoined Manila traffic, though on a foot path. The railed steps were jammed at several places as each line of tourists had to wait for the other to pass before proceeding forward.

I was told however, that up till five years ago, there were hardly any tourists. Then, all of a sudden, the fame of the hanging coffins went viral. Of late, there is a night bus from Manila and another bus service from nearby Baguio bringing busloads of visitors every day. Buses and vans arrive every weekend with young tourists in droves, flooding the 40-minute walk from the Episcopal Church to the coffin site.

It may seem strange, but I myself have been yearning to come here for years, ever since seeing a single picture of these hanging coffins of the Philippines in a magazine over two decades ago. I had studied similar burial customs and hanging coffin sites in China since 1985. The main difference is the burial rite has died in China over 400 years ago, and it is still practiced here in the Philippines.

我在四處遊走的時候，路過的當地人都會跟他揮揮手或者點點頭。

昨天下午我一到薩加達，*Joachim* 就帶我用爬山的方式進入回音谷，這峽谷的懸棺是最出名的。我們抄了聖公會教堂旁邊的一條捷徑，然後直通到懸棺的主要通道。雖然我走的是小步道，但突然間有種回到馬尼拉熱鬧的街道的感覺。護欄階梯有好幾個地方都塞滿了遊客，因為走道太窄一定要等對向的人過後才能繼續向前。

他們告訴我五年前這裡很少有遊客。然後突然間，懸棺的名氣傳開來。最近開始有了夜間巴士從馬尼拉跟附近的碧瑤過來，每天滿載一車又一車的遊客來到這裡。除了巴士，麵包車也每個周末載著大批的年輕遊客前來，塞滿這條從教堂走到懸棺需要四十分鐘的步道。

也許有些奇怪，自從二十年前在一本雜誌上看到一張菲律賓的懸棺照片後，我就一直很想來這裡看看。從一九八五年接觸到中國的懸棺，我研究過類似的葬禮風俗。兩邊最大的不同是，這種風俗在四百年前已經在中國消失，但是依舊存在於菲律賓。

一九九九年我帶領 CERS 去探險，找到從未被發現的懸棺遺址，我們也去保存它。探索頻道為我們的發現做了一個

CERS scaffolding to conserve coffins / CERS coffins site in China · CERS 搭鷹架保護懸棺 / CERS 在中國的懸棺項目點

In 1999, I had led our CERS team to explore and conserve one coffin site we discovered that had never been reported before. A full-hour Discovery Channel film about our work on the hanging coffins of China won Best Documentary Award. Now after twenty-five years of dreaming and two days of driving from Manila, I finally have my five minutes grace with the spirits residing in the hanging coffins of the Philippines!

Alma is owner of the Inandako's B&B, opened three years ago to accommodate the huge influx of tourists. After 25 years as a dentist, she decided to retire early and now enjoys managing her six-room outfit. The bed is spacious and the breakfast sumptuous, a full meal including her famous cream of pumpkin soup, vegetable, egg, corn beef, toast and rice. She is a member of the Igorot tribe who has lived among these karst hills as long as history has a record. This region is called the Cordillera, or Mountain District.

小時的節目，還得了最佳紀錄片的獎項。二十五年的白日夢過去了，從馬尼拉出發兩天的車程後，我終於可以見到住在菲律賓懸棺裡的靈魂了。

Alma 是 *Inandako* 民宿的主人，為了接待大批的遊客，*Inandako* 三年前開始營業。當了二十五年的牙醫後她決定提早退休，現在很開心地經營這個有著六個房間的民宿。床很大，早餐很豐盛，早餐包括有名的南瓜濃湯、蔬菜、蛋、醃牛肉、吐司跟米飯。她是伊哥洛特人，家族已經在這岩溶山丘生活了很久，跟歷史上記錄的一樣久。這個區域叫柯迪勒拉或是山區。

Alma 特別跟我強調伊哥洛特人從來都沒被征服過，隔壁村的獵頭族跟他們很像，但也沒有成功地征服過他們，西班牙人沒有，美國人沒有，二戰時日本人也沒有。唯一只有聖公會征服這裡所有的人，*Alma* 承認，幾乎百分之百的伊哥洛特人都轉信基督教。現在伊哥洛特人過著獨立自治的生活，用傳統的民主方式來處裡社區裡的大小事宜，這傳統遠比許多所謂的民主社會還來的優越。

Alma 非常的熱血也很有自己的主見。她很容易被她覺得不合理的事情惹惱。其中一件事就是懸棺所在地的地名「回音谷」。「根本沒有什麼回音谷，」她一邊說一邊拍桌強調。「導遊們胡亂編個名字，然後來這裡的遊客到了

As Alma noted to me, the Igorot have never been conquered, not by rival neighbor headhunter tribes similar to themselves, not by the Spanish, not by the Americans , and not by the Japanese during WWII. The only conqueror is perhaps the Episcopal Church, which Alma admitted to be almost 100% successful in converting the Igorot people. Even today, the Igorot live a very autonomous existence with a traditional democratic way to manage community affairs and relationships, far superior to many so-called democratic societies.

Alma is very passionate and opinionated. She easily gets irritated by anything she feels is unreasonable. One such matter is the name Echo Valley for the prime site of the coffins. "There is no such place as Echo Valley," she spoke while pounding the dining table in front to make her point. "The guides made

懸棺前都以為可以聽得到回音，真的很討人厭也很不尊重人」，*Alma* 的情緒高漲。

這個衝動的牙醫繼續解釋著這個誤會是怎麼來的。「在我們的傳統裡，這種葬禮只保留給部落裡位高的長者，當有葬禮要舉行的時候，三、四個人會在隊伍前面拿著火把帶隊。他們會一邊走一邊喊逝者的名字好讓祖先知道即將有人加入祂們。」*Alma* 繼續說。因為幾乎所有的伊哥洛特人都是聖公會的教徒，所以牧師也會跟著一起去為逝者祈福。儀式通常在凌晨很早的時候舉行，因為他們相信靈魂這時候是最活躍的。

「過逝的長者會被綁在椅子上，權位越高者，他坐在椅子上的時間就越久，然後才開始進行葬禮。接著將大體捲曲成胎兒狀，放入棺木後再懸掛在崖上。」*Alma* 解釋。這也是為什麼有些棺木相當的短，之前大多數的人猜測可能是小孩子的。男人跟女人都可以葬在懸崖上。有些棺木做成船的形狀。那把椅子也會被掛在棺木外。「我在二零零七年的時候有機會參加了這種葬禮，我把整個儀式都記錄了下來。」*Alma* 驕傲的說。「整個儀式很莊嚴也很有尊嚴！」她的聲音終於溫和了下來。

不過一下子她的聲音又變得高亢，情緒激動，「我痛恨，超痛恨一些情侶會在懸崖腳下大喊『我愛你』，只為了要

up the name and now visitors shout in front of the coffins hoping to hear an echo, and it is just repulsive and disrespectful," Alma said with high emotions.

The fire-brand dentist continued to explain how this misunderstanding came about. "In our tradition, when such a burial ritual takes place, which by the way is only reserved for tribal elders with particularly high standing of rank, three to four persons would lead the way in front of the procession with torches," Alma explained. "As they walked, they would shout out the name of the deceased, allowing the ancestors to know that an important descendent is about to join them," Alma continued. As practically all Igorot belong to the Episcopal Church, a priest would come along to bless the deceased. The entire ritual usually would happen very early in the morning when the spirits are believed to be most active.

"The deceased elder would be bound to a chair, the more senior in rank the longer his body would stay in the chair before burial. The body would be curled into a fetus position and put inside a coffin to be hung up the cliff," Alma explained. That is the reason why some of the coffins are rather short, not for children or infants as many have speculated. Both man or woman can be buried on the cliff. Some coffins are shaped like a boat. The chair would then also be hung outside of the coffin. "I had the opportunity to witness the last burial in 2007 and had it all filmed for my own record," Alma said proudly. "It is a very solemn and respectful ceremony," her voice finally mellowed.

聽到回音。當然，他們是絕對聽不到的！」終於對於回音谷的訓斥結束了。不過那是在我幫腔之前，我說：「別擔心，我會開始散播說，只有在月圓的三更半夜才會聽得到！」這幾天剛好月圓。

沿著河流的懸崖至少有十個懸棺所在地，河流的名字隨著地域而改變，從 Latang 河的山谷到 Alma 家對面的 Dinetaan 河。再沿 Sogong 河往下附近有一個很長的，尚未被命名的洞穴。最受歡迎的回音谷這裡有超過十個棺木，Alma 這邊有四個，然後我發現另一個地點那裡只有一個。

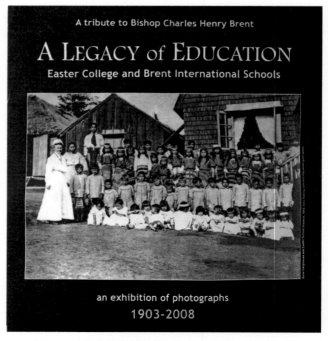

Mission educated Igorot / 西方教會曾為伊哥洛特人興學，此為攝影展紀錄

But only momentarily, as Alma's voice went into high pitch and her mood ballistic again, "I hate it, just hate it, when some tourist with his lover would shout at the bottom of the cliff at the top of his voice 'I love you', to get an echo back. Of course you can never hear the wall talk back." Finally the lecture on Echo Valley ended. But not before I chimed in and said, "Don't worry, I will now circulate the story that it works only at midnight, and during full moon!" After all, it is full moon these couple of days.

There are ten or more coffin sites on the cliff along the river, which changes name as it flows, from Latang River where the gorge is to Dinetaan River where Alma's house faces it. Further down near a long cave it has yet another name - the Sogong River. The most popularly visited site of Echo Valley has more than ten coffins, Alma's site has four, and I noticed an additional site with only one coffin.

With Sagada's new-found fame through the hanging coffins, the indigenous Igorot people have now also become a focus for tourists. A new guideline just issued and posted in public areas can perhaps shed some light on how the Igorot feel about the advent of tourism. While they cherish to some degree the economic gain, they certainly abhor the human and car traffic in tandem with such an influx of outsiders, not to mention some of the behavior of those who look upon their tradition and heritage as either exotic or romantic.

薩加達因為懸棺而出名，連帶原住民伊哥洛特人也被遊客關注。在公共場所張貼新的告示或許可以讓大家了解伊哥洛特人對這些到來的遊客感受是如何。他們在某些程度是珍惜這一點經濟利益，但是他們非常厭惡人類跟汽車帶來大批的外地人，更別說有些遊客的行為，看待原住民的傳統跟遺產好像是很有異國情調的或是浪漫的。

下面是摘錄部分給觀光客的告示，值得留意。

— 禁止觸碰、打擾棺木或是墓地。在沒有取得主持長老直接的授意前，不許試圖加入或是拍攝正在進行的葬禮。

— 請不要問我們「伊哥洛特人在哪裡」。我們就是伊哥洛特人。我們只在特殊場合才會穿傳統的衣服，千萬不要期待我們會穿上傳統的衣服讓你們拍照，我們不做這件事。

— 薩加達是一個社區，不是博物館。如果你想要看我們在一世紀以前生活的樣貌，在邦都有個很棒的博物館，請你去那參觀。別想，也別說我們已經「失去我們的文化」，就只因為我們沒有住在傳統的屋子或是沒有每天穿傳統的服飾。我們也現代化了，受很好的教育，在生活上或是專業領域上都過得很舒服。

Below are a few extracts of the guidelines for tourists, worthy of note:

- Do not touch or disturb coffins or burial sites. Do not attempt to join or film any ritual without direct permission from the presiding elders.

- Please don't ask us "where are the Igorots". We are the Igorots. We do dress in traditional clothing for special occasions, but please don't expect any of us to pose in traditional clothing for pictures, because we don't do that.

- Sagada is a community, not a museum. If you want to see the way we lived a century ago, there's an excellent museum in Bontoc; please visit it. Don't think, or say, that we have "lost our culture" because we no longer live in traditional houses or dress daily in wanes and tapis. We are indigenous people and we are deeply attached to our traditions and culture. We are also modern, well educated people who are comfortable in any living or professional environment the world offers.

- Please conserve water. Sagada suffers from water shortages, especially during dry season and periods of peak tourist flow. This can lead to diversion of water from our farms and rice terraces, where it is desperately needed, to support tourism.

- Please be modest. This is a small, conservative town, and we like it that way. Please save the revealing clothing for the beach, and save the displays of affec-

— 請謹慎用水。薩加達常缺水，尤其是在枯水季跟旅遊旺季。為了支持觀光業，水資源會從我們的農地跟稻米梯田分掉，農業是很需要水的。

— 請你謙虛。這是個小小的，保守的城鎮，我們喜歡這樣。請把暴露的衣服留給海邊，你要表達的愛意留給你自己私人的空間。我們並不是以夜生活出名：商店在薩加達晚上十點關門。如果你想要整晚派對的話也可以，請你去別的地方。這裡沒有性產業，所以請你別浪費時間尋找。

就像 *Joachim* 說的，伊哥洛特人知道生活中什麼是重要的。餐廳跟商店只有在他們想要開的時候營業，可以因為任何原因而關門休息。這些告示很明確地反應伊哥洛特人注重他們的身分跟尊嚴，超過經濟上的利益，這是其他所謂「現代化」世界可以借鏡的。

tion for your private space. We are not known for nightlife: business in Sagada closes at 10PM. If you like to party all night that's fine, but you'll have to do it somewhere else. There is no commercial sex here, so please don't waste your time looking for it.

As Joachim said, the Igorot know their priorities in life. The restaurants and shops are open only when they feel like it, and close for any excuses that come their way. Certainly these guidelines reflect that the Igorot care more about their identity and integrity than economic gain, something the rest of the "modern" world can learn from.

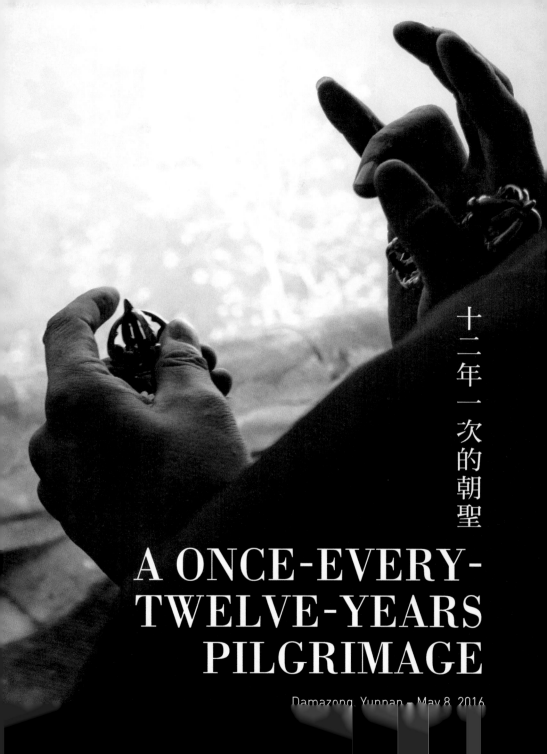

十二年一次的朝聖

A ONCE-EVERY-TWELVE-YEARS PILGRIMAGE

Damazong, Yunnan - May 8, 2016

十二年一次的朝聖

房子旁的公雞早上四點就開始叫了。那是個過早的叫醒服務，但聲音很快就安靜下來了。五點一到公雞又開始叫，這次可是合唱，從附近的山丘傳來，其他的公雞也一起應和。

這裡的公雞都打扮得很體面。牠們絕對不會被送上餐桌，因為牠們是被善意野放的，華人稱「放生」，只不過在這裡善舉是由藏人所為。我們小木屋附近的公雞炫耀著牠們又黑又捲的長尾巴。這裡的公雞被養的很好，都得感謝到達摩祖師洞參拜的佛教徒，他們將大麥撒在山上當成貢品。

人們相信達摩祖師曾在這裡面對懸崖閉關九年直到得道，昇華到佛的境界 *。相傳祂的影子永久地投射在岩壁上。西元五世紀初，達摩是第一位將佛教從印度帶到中國的聖人，祂被視為中國禪宗的第一代祖師。祂的教派演變成禪宗，後來傳播到韓國、日本，甚至還到了歐洲、美國和世界各地。

A ONCE-EVERY-TWELVE-YEARS PILGRIMAGE

The rooster by our house started crowing at 4am. But that may just have been the early morning call, and soon it died down. By 5am, the rooster called again. This time around, there was a chorus from the nearby hill, as other roosters echoed in.

Roosters here are well groomed. They would never be served on the dinner table, as they were released as an act of kindness, what Chinese called "Fang Sheng", meaning "let live". But here it is Tibetans who are performing this act of beneficence. The rooster near our log house sported a long curly black tail. Roosters are all well fed here, thanks to the barley grains scattered all over the top of this mountain as offerings by Buddhist supplicants to Damazong Cave.

Here is where Bodhidharma (Damo in Chinese) is believed to have spent nine years in solitary meditation facing the cliff before he attained nirvana and ascended to the Buddha's world*. It is said that even his shadow can be seen, casted permanently on the rock face. Damo is the sage who first brought Buddhism from India to China during the early part of the 5th century AD, and he is considered the First Patriarch Master of Chinese Chan Buddhism.

達摩祖師是在猴年出生的，剛好今年也是猴年。還有，人們相信祂是在第四個月亮出現的第一天出生，而祂的往生與涅槃，也在同一天，所以這是個吉祥的日子。巧合的是，釋迦牟尼佛也在同一天得到完全的開悟，成為一位佛陀，因此這天成為全世界佛教徒慶祝的日子。

在這個特別的日子，我們停留在這個偏遠又特殊的地方，為了達摩祖師洞閉關室的啟用，這個我們剛剛用了幾個月修復的項目。藏族的朝聖者一大早就開始轉山、祈福。達摩祖師洞穴接近山頂最高處，海拔三千一百公尺高，繞山頂一圈要四十五分鐘還算輕鬆；神山岡仁波齊海拔五千六百公尺，轉山一圈五十三公里；卡瓦格博峰轉山一次需要八天的時間。

＊有其他的傳說提到達摩祖師是在河南省的少林寺裡閉關九年。這也許是少林寺聰明的行銷策略。或許對達摩祖師而言，身為一位先覺者，祂在同一時間身處兩處是件小事。

不到一個鐘頭，我就完成了我的 *kora*，西藏人稱轉山一圈為 *kora*。整條路都被滿滿的經幡裝飾著，有些地方經幡多到你必須蹲下來爬行。據說轉山的次數一定要奇數，如果

His teachings were developed into Zen and later spread throughout Korea and Japan and eventually to Europe, the USA and throughout the world.

Bodhidharma was born during the year of the Monkey, which matches this year's zodiac. Furthermore, he was believed to be born on the First Day of the Fourth Moon, as well as attaining nirvana at his passing away on the same auspicious day. This coincides with the day when Shakyamuni attained full merit and became the Buddha, a day celebrated by Buddhists around the world.

So it is on this very special day that we adjourned here to this remote spot to launch the restored meditation house directly adjacent to Damazong Cave. Tibetan pilgrims also started arriving early in the morning to make prayers and perform the circumambulation of the mountain. As the cave is at an elevation of 3100 meters near the top of the pinnacle of a mountain, the circuit around the top is a relatively easy 45 minutes trek, compared to the more strenuous circuit at Kailash of 53 kilometers at near 5600 meters, or the 8-day trek around Khawakarpo.

---

* Other accounts state that Boddhidharma mediated for 9 years at Shaolin Monastery in what is now Henan Province. This may just be an early example of Shaolin's famous marketing savvy. Or perhaps it was Damo after all, as an

Prostrating pilgrims / 磕長頭的朝聖者

enlightened being such as he might find it a simple matter to be in two places at once.

I did my kora, as Tibetans call such a circuit, and finished in slightly over an hour. The entire route was adorned with prayer flags, at some location so thick that one had to crawl under them. It is said that one must make the Kora in odd numbers. If you were to make two circuits, it would be advisable to finish a third one, a fifth one, a seventh one, or so on and so forth. The most devoted would prostrate up the mountain, as well as prostrate around the circuit. Each circuit would then require a long day of repeated kneeling, prostrating flat on the ground, standing, then taking three steps forward before repeating the same routine. I conveniently stopped at a single digit single circuit, on foot.

Our new project came about in a subtle way as if by coincidence, like most other CERS projects. Since 2003, I have passed by the foothill of this mountain several times each year. Looking up at the temple slightly below the peak, I had contemplated making the half day hike 'one of these days,' but never made the time or effort. Then a fire descended upon the temple in 2014 and the government decided to build a road and reconstruct the temple, rushing to finish in time for the 2016 major pilgrimage.

Finally, our own CERS project manifested itself last summer when I was

你打算轉兩圈的話，你會被勸告最好轉三圈，五圈，七圈，以此類推。最虔誠的信徒還會用五體跪拜（磕長頭）的方式上山跟轉山。跪下，全身臥平在地上，站起來，往前走三步，再跪下，全身臥平在地上，再站起來，再往前走三步……一直重複這樣的動作，直到轉山結束。這樣的轉山相對要付出更多的時間。我轉完一圈後就趁此打住，而我還是只用雙腳轉山的。

這個新的項目是以一種微妙的方式讓我們遇見的，完全是個巧合，我們做的項目好像都是這樣。從二零零三年開始，我每年都會經過這山腳下好幾次。往上看著這個在山峰下方一點的寺廟，心裡想著「總有一天」我要花半天的時間來爬這座山，不過從沒實現過。二零一四年，一把火波及這寺廟，政府決定為這裡鋪路並重建寺廟，並且趕著要在二零一六年盛大的朝聖之前完工。

去年夏天我陪同一群年輕的實習生到我們金絲猴／傈僳族的項目所在地，達摩祖師洞的項目就這樣現身了，那裏離這裡不到一個鐘頭的車程。我去過那項目好幾十次，這次我脫隊，開車走在一條剛鋪好的路前往達摩祖師洞。

參觀完這剛修復的寺廟，我留意到有一間殘破的屋子懸在陡峭的山壁上，緊鄰著正在被重建的主要洞穴。從這裡看出去的長江真是壯觀，幾乎轉了個大圓圈，然後流

joining a group of young interns to visit our Golden Monkey/Lisu Hill Tribe project site barely an hour away. Having been to that site dozens of times, I took a break from the group and drove up the newly finished road to visit Damazong Cave.

After visiting the restored temple, I noticed a dilapidated house over the steep hill, directly adjacent to the presiding cave structure being reconstructed. It had a most awe inspiring view of the Yangtze meandering below and into the distant hills. The modest building turned out to be a meditation house belonging to a Tibetan teacher monk.

A lone construction worker present gave the name of Monk Gongjiu who was teaching young monks at a school half way down the mountain. We went down the hill in search. The humble monk was most hospitable and over a bowl of butter tea, we discussed the possibilities of restoring the meditation house with leaking roof and badly in need of repair. Soon an agreement was struck that CERS would take on this new project and make the building usable again before the 2016 pilgrimage began.

Subsequent trips over the next few months took this house to its current status, including kitchen, bathrooms, incense burner, observation deck, and an extension log house detailed with religious objects for visiting monks to use as a meditation facility. There is also a small dorm area for visiting students to

Deck of meditation house / 閉關室前的平台

入遠方的山裡。這間屋子原來是位藏族和尚老師所擁有
的閉關室。

工地裡唯一一位工人告訴我們，擁有這間閉關室的和尚
叫貢秋，他在半山腰那裏的佛學院教導年輕的和尚。我
們於是下山找人。謙卑的和尚非常好客，我們一邊喝著
酥油茶一邊討論修復閉關室的可能，破舊的小屋連屋頂
也開始漏水，迫切地需要好好整修一番。很快的，和尚
同意讓 CERS 接手這項目，讓房子可以在二零一六年的
朝聖日前修復好。

Distant hills / 遠方的河谷

use in the future such that they could learn about the traditional practices of Tibetan Buddhism through this important religious site.

As I left the CERS restored Damazong meditation house the day after my pilgrimage, I nodded to myself in approval that this is yet another small project that we undertook in record time, yet with lasting value to many who would come after us. I too, may come back for a span of meditation when I am retired.

But for now, I feel most gratified that as of today, Tashi Rinpoche, a close friend of CERS and a descendent of the 7th Dalai Lama's family, would begin

接下來幾個月的時間，房子變成現在的樣子：廚房、浴室、焚香爐、觀景工作台，以及一間延伸的小木屋，木屋裡有宗教性的裝飾品，可以給來訪的和尚當作閉關的空間。也有一小間宿舍可以給來這裡的學生使用，他們可以在這個重要的宗教聖地學習傳統藏傳佛教的習俗。

朝聖後我離開 CERS 修復的達摩祖師洞閉關室，我很滿意這又是一件打破紀錄的小項目，它竟能在這麼短的時間完成，然而這房子所保留下的價值是久遠的。也許在我退休之後我會回來這裡閉關冥想。

我很欣慰，札西活佛，CERS 的好友，第七達賴喇嘛家族的後代，就從今天起在我們剛修復好的這個木屋裡開始一個月的閉關。我希望在札西活佛之後，還會有許多虔誠的信徒繼續來這裡利用這個很特別又吉祥的宗教設施。

（達摩祖師洞閉關室修復項目是由 Margot and Thomas Pritzker 家族基金會與 CERS 共同合作）

his month-long meditation at our newly restored house. It is my hope that Tashi would only be the first of many such devotees who can make use of this very special and auspicious religious retreat.

(The Damazong Meditation House restoration project is co-supported by the Margot and Thomas Pritzker Family Foundation and CERS)

House framed by prayer flags / 被經幡圍繞的房子

A NINE-DAY CIRCUIT AROUND THE PLATEAU

Zhongdian, Yunnan – May 19, 2016

環行高原九天的旅程

環行高原九天的旅程

「快把它收起來，它會讓你惹上麻煩的！」堪布一邊將照片塞回給我，一邊低聲跟我說。那是一張達賴喇嘛在他達蘭薩拉的家中接見我的照片。我並不是對政治不敏感，我從一九七四年就開始在中國工作，也經歷過部分的文化大革命，我知道怎麼拿捏其中方寸，但堪布卻不知道。基於對他的尊重我把照片塞進羽絨夾克內層的口袋裡。

不過這個小插曲為我們在西藏高原，這個非常偏遠的角落打開了一扇門，也可能是好幾扇門。琼柯寺位在青海與四川交界的西藏自治區裡的小角落。直到不久前，都沒有道路通往這個寺廟，要來這裡需要騎上好幾天的馬。不過現在有一條吊橋連結四川偏遠的洛須鎮跟這個寺廟。

以前洛須鎮是四川省的一個窮鄉僻壤，在長江上游，是鄧柯縣的縣府所在地，一九七八年被取消，併到鄰近的兩個縣，德格縣跟石渠縣裡，主要的原因是因為它太偏遠了。這樣也好，因為直到二十世紀後期的幾十年，這個區域還是非常原始的部落。鄧柯區是西藏傑出英雄嶺

A NINE-DAY CIRCUIT AROUND THE PLATEAU

"Put this away, it may cause you trouble," the Abbot whispered as he slipped back the picture to me. I was showing him a picture of the Dalai Lama receiving me at his home in Dharamsala. I am no stranger to political sensitivity, having worked in China since 1974 and through part of the Cultural Revolution. I know what I can get away with, but not the Abbot. Out of consideration, however, I stuck the picture inside the inner pocket of my down jacket.

But that short episode opened the door, or doors, at this remotest corner on the Tibetan plateau. Qiongguo Monastery is located inside Tibet, but at a faraway corner where Qinghai and Sichuan meet with the Tibetan Autonomous Region. Until recently, no road penetrated into this monastery except one that required days of horseback riding. Today, a suspension bridge connects the distant town of Luoxu on the Sichuan side to the monastery.

Luoxu itself was once the capitol of a backwater county of Sichuan called Dengke along the upper Yangtze that was disbanded in 1978, due largely to its remoteness, and integrated into the two nearby counties of Dege and

格薩爾王的家鄉，嶺格薩爾王最得意的將軍鄧馬就是從洛須鎮來的。

因為這個原因，這個長江對面的寺廟全名是鄧馬琼柯寺。這間寺廟可不是普通的喇嘛寺。傳說這間寺廟跟宗喀巴大師，也是黃教的創立者有直接的關係。祂的大弟子奉命建立幾間寺廟。大師將袈裟丟進長江裡，並預言袈裟停留的地方就是未來蓋寺廟的地點，結果袈裟順水而下停在現在琼柯寺的位置。琼柯在藏語的意思正是袈裟。

我們到的時候剛好碰到寺廟的辯經，對我們團隊來說這

Serxu. It might as well be, since the region was extremely tribal until the last few decades of the 20th Century. The Dengke region was the home of the most brilliant Tibetan hero and fiercest warrior, King Gesar of Ling. And the town of Luoxu is where Dengma, his top general, came from.

For that reason the full name of the monastery across the Yangtze is Dengma Qiongguo Monastery. This however is not just any Tibetan lamasery. Legend has it that this monastery was directly related to Tsongkhapa, founder of the Yellow Hat or Gelug Sect. His lead disciple was commissioned to start a number of monasteries. Casting his monk's robe into the Yangtze, he prophesized that the robe would stop at the future site of an important monastery. The robe floated downriver and ended up at the current location of Qiongguo monastery, thus the name, which means monk's robe in Tibetan.

Our arrival coincided with the monastic debate week and my team was treated to an exciting morning of activities followed by mass chanting in the covered courtyard of the main assembly hall, a building that miraculously survived the Cultural Revolution, possibly due to its remoteness. Silang Puji, the chief abbot, was presiding at the function, sitting inside the Assembly Hall in front of the altar, with the Buddhist statues and deities high above.

My photo introduction seemed to work. I asked to purchase a monk's robe, namesake of the monastery, as a religious relic for our newly finished museum

是一個非常有意思的活動，能在寺廟前的中庭裡看著僧眾辯經，以及之後聽著他們誦經。這棟建築物奇蹟似的歷經了文化大革命後留存下來，也許是因為它真的夠偏遠。四朗培吉堪布坐在大殿裡貢有佛像跟神明的佛龕前主持法會。

見面時我拿出來的照片好像發揮了功用。我詢問是否可以買一件袈裟，作為我們在中甸中心剛完工的博物館的文物收藏，因為袈裟剛好是這寺廟的名字。「我會把我的袈裟給你。」堪布輕聲說。他抓著我的手帶我走幾步到佛龕旁的一張高椅前，他將披掛在椅背上的藏紅袈裟遞給我。我要付錢給他，但是他卻只搖了搖頭。

「別露出來！」他警惕我。很快的我的羽絨夾克變得更臃腫了，我夾帶著袈裟走出大殿。四朗培吉不是一般的高僧或堪布。他的家族可以追溯到幾個世紀前藏傳佛教格魯派的開始。他對寺廟裡的和尚很嚴格，有超過二十間分散在各地的屬寺，都附屬於他這間之下，全都採用跟這裡一樣嚴謹的規定。

瓊柯寺是這趟考察最遠的地點也是最令人興奮的。我研究長江，在這裡來來回回遊走超過三十年，包括三次去到這區域的河流源頭，可是這是我第一次跨過長江來到這個三個省分交集的地方。從青海到四川的這段以上叫

chapel at our Zhongdian Center. "I will give you my robe," whispered the abbot. He took me by the hand and paced the few steps to the high chair by the altar, took off the saffron robe draped over its back and passed it to me. I offered to pay him and he simply shook his head.

"Don't show it," he cautioned. Soon my down jacket took on a more plumpish appearance as I walked out of the Assembly Hall. Silang Puji is not just any high monk or abbot. His family pedigree hailed back centuries to the beginning of the Gelug Sect of Tibetan Buddhism. His discipline for the monks of his monastery is so straight that over twenty other monasteries far and wide decided to become the sub-monasteries of Qiongguo Monastery and adopted his same stringent rules and regulations.

Qiongguo monastery is the farthest destination for me on this short yet exciting expedition. Having studied and crisscrossed the Yangtze for over three decades, including reaching the source region on three occasions, this is the first time I arrive, and cross, the Yangtze where three provinces meet. This is also where the Tongtianhe changes its name to Jinshajiang as the river flows from Qinghai into Sichuan. We set camp for the night at the confluence.

After a night and morning of snowstorm, we exited the region. On the way out, we stopped by a hot spring by the roadside. The name is Duojenri, phonetically and appropiately meaning "lots of praise in hotness" in Chinese.

通天河，從這裡開始成為金沙江，我們今晚就在這交接點處紮營。

經過一整夜跟一早上的暴風雪後，我們離開了這裡。途中在路邊的溫泉暫停，這個溫泉叫「*Duojenri*」，發音跟意思在中文是「多讚熱」。水溫燙到沒有辦法洗澡，所以我們只好泡泡腳。不一會兒溫泉旁的屋子裡走出一位年輕的女士，我心想她可能是來收錢的。結果不是，這溫泉完全免費。泡完腳後，我探頭進去這屋子裡跟這女士的父親見面。

六十五歲的格榮曲秋看起來過的很好，他是個商人，靠賣大麥跟一些商品賺了錢。一袋袋的穀物裝在老舊但卻堅固的皮革旅行袋內，被堆疊在牆邊，那種袋子現在已經沒人

Tent in snow / Moving through snowstorm · 雪中的帳篷 / 在暴風雪中前進

The water was way too hot to take a bath, so we satiated ourselves by dipping our feet in. Soon a young lady came out of the house next to the spring. I thought there must be a fee charged. No, it turned out to be absolutely free for all. Upon finishing with the treat for our feet, I poked my head into the house and met the father of the lady.

Sixty-five years old Gerong Qucho turned out to be quite well to do, having amassed a small fortune as a local trader in barley grain and other merchandise. Against the wall were stacked sacks of grain stored in old and sturdy leather caravan bags used no more today. I tried to negotiate to get a pair for our collection, but the price was prohibitive, running into the thousands. Next I saw a large yak blanket used to cover another stack of merchandises on the floor. Gerong wanted 1500Rmb, the equivalent of US$200. It was time to grease the deal with my secret and sacred weapon of the Dalai Lama again.

Seeing that the family altar had a picture of the Karmapa, I doubled down with another few pictures I took while attending the Enthronement of the Karmapa in Tibet in 1992 when he was seven years old, coupled with a picture I took of him as a tall adult standing next to me when I visited him in Dharamsala. It worked. The price dropped immediately by half to 800Rmb.

In passing, I asked if there were still sitting/sleeping mats made from musk

在用了。我嘗試著想買一對做為我們的收藏，但是價錢太高，要好幾千塊。接著我看到一大張氂牛毯在地上，用來覆蓋商品。格榮開價人民幣一千五百塊，相當於美金兩百元。是時候把神聖的秘密武器－達賴喇嘛拿出來用了。

我看到他家族神龕上有一張噶瑪巴的照片，於是我拿出幾張一九九二年噶瑪巴坐牀大典時的我為他所拍的照片，那時噶瑪巴才七歲；還有幾張是在達蘭薩拉時他站在我旁邊，長大成人後的樣子，他長得很高大。照片奏效。價錢馬上降了將近一半，只要人民幣八百塊錢。

我順便問道有沒有用麝毛做的坐墊或是睡墊。要找到這東西幾乎是不可能，因為在高原上的鹿差不多都被捕光了，珍貴的麝香曾經是一種傳統的藥材也是香水業必用的原料。

西藏人相信麝毛做的墊子可以防風濕，只有貴族跟位高的喇嘛才用得上。製作一個完整的墊子需要一百隻以上的麝。麝的毛很獨特，長的像軟木塞，中空，這樣的毛髮讓麝可以在濕冷的喜瑪拉雅山上保暖。

出人意料，格榮說他有一件這樣的墊子。這一件非常大，也很有年份。他正準備要用剪刀開個口，好讓我看看裡面的內容物，但是我找到一個縫隙看到露出來的針線。果真這是黃色的野生動物的毛，不是棉或是其他衣料。

deer hair stuffed in between fabric layers. This is a most unlikely item to find, as the source animal has almost totally disappeared throughout the plateau due to depletion of the animal for its valuable musk, once a key ingredient for traditional medicine and the perfume industry alike.

Tibetans believe mats made from musk deer hair will prevent rheumatism, and these were only commonly used by royalty and high lamas. It may take upwards of 100 musk deer to yield enough hair to make one full size mat. The hair of the musk deer is unique, with a cork-screw shape and hollow center that must help keep the animal warm in the cold wet climate of the high Himalayas.

Surprisingly, Gerong revealed that he had one such mat. It turned out to be an extremely large and very old specimen. He was ready with a scissors to cut open a corner to show me the contents, but I had already found a section where old stitches were falling, revealing the inside. Indeed there was yellowish wild hair showing, not cotton or cloth stuffing. I wanted to recondition it to serve as a sitting/sleeping pad for high monks who would soon begin to use our Buddhist chapel attached to the new museum we are finishing at our Zhongdian Center. Through some hard negotiating, the price dropped from 6000 Rmb to 2700, with my sacred pictures changing hands to sit over his altar.

我想要把它放在中甸中心的經堂讓以後到那裡的高僧使用，不管是當成坐墊還是睡墊。未來，經堂會在我們剛完工的博物館旁邊。經過好一番的討價還價之後，價錢從人民幣六千降到兩千七百元，我贈送的幾張神聖的照片也掛在神龕上了。

這趟行程我忙著拍照、蒐集資料和跟寺廟、路邊攤還有經過營區的當地人商討收購文物。團隊裡好幾位成員也忙著購買冬蟲夏草，蟲草在過去這二十年改變了整個西藏高原的經濟樣貌。只要跟這產業有一點點關係的人都賺了錢，從產地到中國的城市，到香港跟外國的市場都為這個被賜福的真菌感染的昆蟲瘋狂。價錢最近從最高價，超過人民幣一百塊錢一根開始狂跌，跌到最大的一根賣人民幣三十元，中尺寸的賣二十元，賣相差一點的只要人民幣五元。

就在一天前我們在雅礱江的河岸，這是四條在四川流進長江的其中一條河流（四川的意思是「四條河流」）。地理上長江跟雅礱江相隔差不多只有六十公里跟一個山脊之遠。兩條河流有點平行地往下流，下一個交會點是在直線距離八百公里處。我們在雅礱江的河岸紮營，海拔三千八百五十公尺，鄰近有另一個很少人知道的哲嘎寺，屬於寧瑪派（紅教），寺裡有超過四百位和尚。

Back on the road during the times while I was busy with photography, data collecting, or artifact negotiation from monasteries, roadside stands and campsite passers-by, a number of our team members were busy negotiating and buying cordyceps, the caterpillar fungus that has transformed the entire economic landscape of the Tibetan plateau over the last two decades. Fortunes were made by anyone even remotely connected to this business, driving a craze from source to markets in China's big cities, Hong Kong and overseas for these tiny heaven-endowed, fungusinfected worms. Prices have dropped recently from a high of over 100Rmb per piece to barely 30 for large specimens and 20 for medium sized ones, or even 5 for an ugly tiny worm.

Just the day before, we were at the bank of the Yalong River, one of four rivers that feed the Yangtze in Sichuan (Sichuan meaning 'four rivers'). Geographically the upper reaches of both the Yangtze and the Yalong here are separated by only roughly 60 kilometers and one ridge. Flowing south somewhat in parallel to each other, they won't join each other for another 800 kilometers further south as the crow flies. We camped at the bank of the Yalong, here at an elevation of 3850 meters, by another little-known monastery, Drekar, of the Nyingma (Red) Sect with over 400 monks.

A young girl of 22 by the name of Nimaco was most lively and proactive, offering to show us a nunnery nearby. Driving along the Yalong and then through some twists and turns up the mountain, we located inside a valley the

Mute nun silhouette / 八關齋戒中的阿尼

hidden nunnery by the same name of Drekar. This nunnery, standing at 4020 meters elevation and affiliated with the monastery, has less than forty nuns. None were in sight, but the presiding Khempo (head monk) Bienma showed us the main hall. Mumbling some noises through his nose, we finally figured out that all nuns, as well as himself, were observing the 8-day Mute Prayer ritual, which forbid them to leave their abode and restricted their talk. I peeked through one window and saw a quiet nun in her meditation routine.

Without planning, this expedition became a monastic pilgrimage, visiting new "old" monasteries for the first time as well as revisiting three old "old" monasteries that were all previous CERS project sites. For some reason, I love small and remote monasteries, in particular one suspended in mid air, and generally feel turned off by large monasteries, especially those that are enshrined with gold and sparkle brightly, shining down on me. The full glare of such "monumental" buildings made me turn my head away somewhat in disgust. Two monasteries I passed by, Litang and Juqing, both considered schools of highest learning for Tibetan Buddhism in Kham, are such examples.

I could not help imagining that such glitter and excess were fueled by the nouveau riche who showered these religious sites with money, much of it ill-gotten, as a way of redeeming themselves. Today, if they offered enough, a hall would be built for any supplicant, I suppose. Yes, maybe monasteries are

二十二歲的女孩 Nimaco，非常活潑也很主動，她問我們想不想去附近的尼姑寺看看。我們於是沿著雅礱江行駛，在山上經歷些轉折後，終於到了隱藏在山谷裡的尼姑寺，這間也叫哲嘎。這間尼姑寺位於海拔四千零二十公尺，不到四十位尼姑，但都不見她們，只有堪布 Khempo Bienma 帶我們去大殿。他從鼻子發出一些喃喃聲，我們後來才知道原來所有的尼姑，包括這位堪布正在進行為期八天的禁聲啞巴經，期間他們不可以離開住所，不可以說話。我從一個窗戶往裡面探，看到一位尼姑很安靜地在做例行的冥想。

出發時並沒有這樣的計畫，但是這次的考察似乎成了寺廟的朝聖之旅，參觀了我們從未去過的、新的「舊」寺廟；還有去了三座舊的「舊」寺廟，也是 CERS 以前的項目點。不知道是什麼原因，我特別喜愛位在偏遠地方，小小的寺廟，更有一所是懸在半空中的；通常我對大寺廟沒有什麼好感，尤其是那種供奉黃金，對著我閃閃發亮的。對那種令人炫目的、「雄偉的」建築物，我很不以為然。我路過康區的理塘長青春科爾寺跟德格竹慶寺兩間寺廟，它們就是這種寺廟；但是這兩間可是被視為藏傳佛教最高等的學府呵。

我忍不住想像暴發戶給這些寺廟大筆大筆的鈔票，把寺廟搞得閃亮亮的，他們把捐錢當作贖罪的一種方式，因為很

places for cleansing one's soul and mind. But it is not the original purpose of these pantheons of religious worship to be patronizing to those with deep pockets, or be corrupted by people eager to pledge support in order to launder their souls.

By comparison, all three CERS monastic sites we had the good fortune to revisit and stay at are small and special. Renkang, despite being the house where the 7th Dalai Lama was born, retains its historic old look and humbleness as if taking us back four centuries in time. Lumorab or Tumu monastery, where we constructed small dams and retaining walls to contain

多錢是來路不明的。我想如果他們捐的夠多，還可以用他們的名義蓋個大殿。也是，寺廟是讓一個人潔淨靈魂和心靈的地方。不過這並不是宗教的原意，這樣會對口袋深的人有差別待遇，或是被這些急切想要用金錢去救贖靈魂的人繼續腐化。

相較之下 CERS 的這三個寺廟項目顯得小又獨特，這趟我們剛好有幸重返的這三個地方看看。儘管是七世達賴喇嘛出生的屋子，仁康古屋還是保存它歷史的樣貌跟質樸，好像可以把我們帶回四個世紀以前。我們也在土木寺建造小水壩跟檔土牆來保護大殿上方的泥石流，而這偏遠的寺廟依舊還是很幽靜。它的壁畫也保存的很好，在寧瑪派寺廟裡算是數一數二的。

最後是薩迦派（白教）的白雅寺，這座寺廟對 CERS 跟我來說是很親密的。一九八零年代當我第一次見到白雅活佛就跟他成為很好的朋友。他好幾次為了宗教的典禮來香港我都接待了他。雖然這次我們來拜訪時他身在成都，但是他的堪布 Zangyang Tsecun 非常地好客，堅持我們一定要在這裡過夜。我們的調研人員第一次來到這裡是在一九九一年的春天，當時還下著雪，接下來的好幾年國際團隊陸續來到這裡修復房子跟壁畫。

十年前進出白雅寺要騎上四天的馬。不過隨著中國的富

a landslide above the assembly hall, continues to be remote and pristine. Its mural remains in great condition and is one of the best among Nyingma Sect monasteries.

Lastly, Baiya Monastery of the Sakya (White Sect) is very intimate to CERS and me. Baiya Rinpoche has become a very close personal friend since we first met in the 1980s. I have entertained him on several occasions when he visited Hong Kong to perform religious ceremonies. Although he was away in Chengdu during our current visit, his chief abbot Zangyang Tsecun was extremely hospitable and insisted that we must stay for the night. This is the site where our first survey team moved in during the snowy spring of 1991, with subsequent international teams staying through several seasons to restore the building and murals.

Entering and exiting Baiya Monastery even ten years ago would have required four days of travel... on horseback. But today, with China's new gained wealth, and corresponding technological prowess, most of the dirt roads and treks of the past are now paved. Before I left Baiya, the Rinpoche called his Abbot and instructed him to remove the gigantic saffron monk's robe draping the presiding seated Buddha. Wrapped in beautiful embroidered fabric, the sacred robe was his gift for us to adorn our newly finished chapel at our Zhongdian Museum. So for now, I have not one, but two special monk's robe that would accompany us back home to our Center in Yunnan.

裕，還有進步的技術實力，現在大部分的土石路都鋪設好了。離開白雅寺前活佛打了電話給堪布，指示他把垂掛在佛陀上的巨大藏紅袈裟拿下來。袈裟包裹在很漂亮的繡布裡，這件神聖的袈裟是活佛送給我們的禮物，給我們裝飾中甸中心剛完工的博物館。所以現在我不只有一件，我有兩件很特別的袈裟要帶回去我們在雲南的中心。

有三個晚上我們借宿在鍾愛的寺廟裡，這是很珍貴的經驗，不過我也很珍惜在高山上，在高大的冷杉和松樹林間露營度過的五個夜晚。一陣暴風雪後天空變得好藍，暮光下我的心神享受著大自然的美好。每天吃著自己在營區煮的飯，喝著山泉水，這樣的日子已經超過一個星期了。我們該回家了，但是大自然的甜美還縈繞著我，我將永遠渴望回到這裡。

Abbot Zangyang / 住持 Zangyang

While the three nights' stay at our beloved monasteries were gems for the heart, I also cherish the five nights we spent camping out in high mountains and among tall fir and pine forests. From a sudden snow blizzard to idyllic blue sky and twilight, my mind feasted on nature to the fullest. For over a week, we ate meals cooked in camp and drank from mountain springs. Though it is now time to go home, that sweetness of nature lingers and I will always be longing to return.

Baiya monatery / 白雅寺

Monk on bike / 摩托車上的僧人

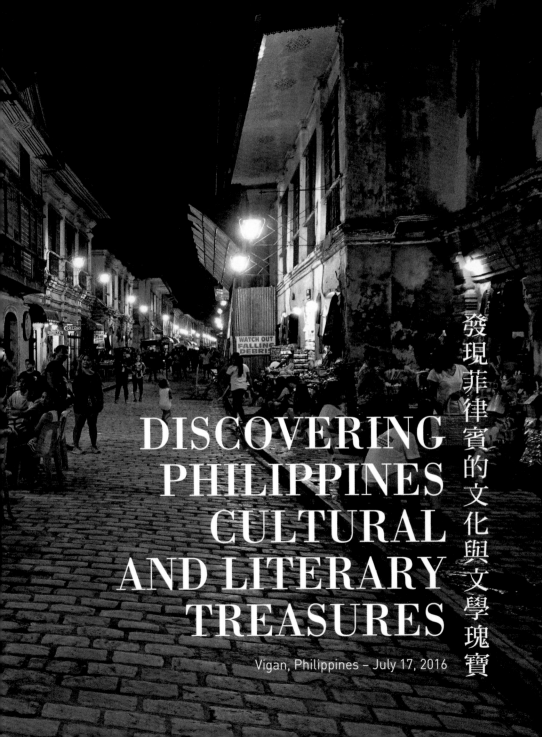

DISCOVERING PHILIPPINES CULTURAL AND LITERARY TREASURES

Vigan, Philippines – July 17, 2016

發現菲律賓的文化與文學瑰寶

發現菲律賓的文化與文學瑰寶

——與佛朗西斯科 · 塞爾尼 · 荷西一起的旅行

新當選的菲律賓總統杜特蒂在他精簡扼要的就職演說中引用三個人的名字，其中兩位是美國人——林肯跟羅斯福。唯一一位他提到的菲律賓人就是佛朗西斯科 · 塞爾尼 · 荷西。塞爾尼的朋友都叫他「*Frankie*」，他是菲律賓國寶級的文學家，也是享譽國際的作家。在他得獎的許多小說裡，都可以看到他堅毅不妥協的政治和社會立場，他的作品已經被翻譯成二十幾種語言。

也許有人不會總是認同塞爾尼寫的，但是他不會因此去修飾他有時過於激進的觀點，所以某些他的敵人還是很尊敬他。大部分的原因是他敢言，也敢寫的個性。這種個性是把雙刃劍，在太平時代對他有利；在亂世卻很容易帶來麻煩。在菲律賓這樣的地方，你可以預期他遇到比較多的狀況是後者。

在馬可仕總統任內戒嚴的十二年裡，有四年塞爾尼的護照是被扣走的，他被禁止踏出國門。在被壓迫的恐怖年代他

DISCOVERING PHILIPPINES CULTURAL AND LITERARY TREASURES – *a journey with Sionil Jose*

Newly-minted President Duterte of the Philippines quoted three persons in his concise and succinct inaugural speech, two of them from America - Abraham Lincoln and Franklin D. Roosevelt. Only one person was mentioned from his own country - Francisco Sionil Jose. Sionil, known to his friends as "Frankie," is a National Artist of the Philippines and an internationally renowned author with an uncompromising political and social stand, as illustrated in his many award-winning novels, some translated into over twenty languages worldwide.

One may not always agree with Sionil's writing, at times abrasive and with progressive to radical viewpoints, nonetheless he is respected even by some of his enemies. This is due largely to his dare-say-it, as well as darewrite-it, character. That personality is a double-edged sword, serving him well in times of peace, and creating problems for the writer in more turbulent times. In a place like the Philippines, one can expect more of the latter than the former.

For four years during the twelve-year martial law period of President Marcos'

Beautiful church / Church in Rosales · 美麗的教堂 / 羅薩萊斯都的教堂

rule, Sionil had his passport taken away and was restrained from traveling outside of the country. There was even a time of terror when he did not dare sleep at home, but found refuge during the night at a friend's home. What bewildered and hurt him most was when he found out that he was blacklisted through the betrayal by one of his close friends. Twice he mentioned that to me. Both times his voice went dim. A prolific writer, his novels addressing the unjust social order in his country were read widely by the literati and intellectuals, a candle of light in the darkness - political darkness - of an era in contemporary Philippines history.

But how was that character trait formed? A trip with Sionil to his hometown and the region where he grew up may reveal part of the answers. He reminded me repeatedly that he is 91 years old. So when my Palawan project hit a rock, I took his invitation as a consolation prize and traveled with Sionil to the northern Philippines to the town where he spent his childhood. Little did I know that the trip would turn out to be more than a prize.

Rosales is a small town by the scale of Manila or Hong Kong, from where I had just come. I can image how much smaller it must have been almost a century ago when Sionil was born there in 1924. The town today would not provide much lingering memories for Frankie, as now there are too many McDonald's, Jollibees and SevenElevens around. With Sionil's instruction, his driver took us directly to the Rosales Elementary School. Here he recounted

甚至不敢睡在家裡，只能窩在朋友家避難。最讓他想不透也最傷心的是，他被列在黑名單的原因竟然是親密好友的背叛。這件事他跟我提了兩次，兩次他的聲音都變得黯淡。他作品豐富，並且被文人和知識分子廣泛地閱讀，他的小說經常寫到在自己國家發生的不公不義，他的文字就像是黑暗政治中的一盞蠟燭，敘述的是一段菲律賓的近代史。

到底他的性格是怎麼形成的？跟塞爾尼去一趟他長大的地方就可以知道。他提醒我好幾次他已經九十一歲了。所以當我在巴拉望的項目遇到困難時，我把他的邀請當作是安慰自己的獎賞，他邀我一起去北菲律賓他小時候住的地

that, while attending fourth grade, he encountered spirits, or "dwarfs", under the space between the school building and the ground. While retrieving a football dropped under the building, he found three tiny old fellows with wrinkled faces and eyes like burning charcoal. That memory stayed with him throughout his life. Climbing the water tower to look at the town from above was another adventure of the young boy.

Though our stay at Rosales was short, Sionil took the opportunity to drop off stacks of books at a neighboring private school that was lacking reading material in its library. He was obviously proud of the Ilocano rural and agrarian society, yet has written about the peasantry being tyrannized. As we drove, he looked lovingly at the rice fields by the roadside, as a new planting season had just begun. Occasionally we stopped to pick up his favorite popsicle or cone ice-cream.

At one point, I asked Sionil what other names he could come up with that have become an adjective in the English language. I cited Platonic and Orwellian as examples. He quickly came up with Quixotic. I argued that Don Quixote is only an imagined person, not a real name, so our game continued. I happened to bring two T-shirts, which I planned to wear in alternation. Both have Don Quixote imprinted on their front, a perfect coincidence, as Sionil has admired the author Cervantes since his early writing days. He even described how Cervantes affected his own writing during a lecture he delivered at a

Sionil at his school / 賽爾尼曾就讀的小學

方。我根本不知道這趟旅行結果會比我想像中的還棒。

不論是對馬尼拉或者我來自的香港來說，羅薩萊斯都只是個小鎮。我可以想像將近一百年前，塞爾尼出生的一九二四年，這個村莊一定還更小。這個城鎮今天不會帶給 Frankie 多少年幼時的回憶，因為現在滿街有麥當勞，Jollibees 跟 7-11。在塞爾尼的指示下他的司機把我們直接帶到羅薩萊斯小學。在這裡他回憶起四年級的時候，他在校舍跟地面中間遇見了精靈，也或許是「小矮人」。足球掉進校舍底下，當他跑去撿的時候卻看見了三個滿臉皺紋的小矮人，眼睛就像的燒得火紅的木炭。這是他一輩子都忘不了的記憶。爬到水塔上俯看整個城鎮，也是那個小男孩的另一個冒險故事。

雖然我們在羅薩萊斯只做短暫的停留，但是塞爾尼利用這機會把一疊又一疊的書交給附近的一間私立學校，因為他們圖書館的藏書不多。很顯然的他對伊洛卡諾鄉村跟附近的農業社會感到驕傲，他也曾經寫過農民被壓迫，被蠻橫對待的故事。開車的時候他心滿意足的望著路邊的稻田，新的一季種植才剛開始。偶爾我們會停下車來買他最喜歡的冰棒或是冰淇淋。

一度我問塞爾尼，有哪些人的名字在英文裡面已經變成形容詞了。我舉柏拉圖跟歐威爾為例。他很快的回答唐吉軻

Cervantes Lecture Series at the University of Santo Tomas, where Sionil graduated many decades ago. Founded in 1611, Santo Tomas is the oldest university in Asia.

At every town we passed by on the way north, we stopped and visited churches, some older, some newer. The most impressive were those from the three hundred some odd years of the Spanish rule. Soon all the churches and their names eluded me and gave me spiritual indigestion, though Sionil had them memorized as part of his mental dictionary. I however remember that the Church of Our Lady of the Assumption, better known as the Santa Maria Church at Ilocos Sur, was the most imposing. It was first built in 1765, from brick and mortar with a separate bell tower, and was designated a UNESCO World Heritage Site in 1993.

Sionil's knowledge of the history of Spanish rule, United States rule, and the Second World War and how each affected the region was all new to me. Pointing to the mountain passes along the Cordilleras to our east, he recounted skirmishes of various armies, not the least the more recent ones with the NPA or New People's Army, the largest insurgent group in the country.

We made a stop at Sarrat, a town made famous by hosting the birth place of President Marcos. I visited briefly the house with a few exhibits. Sionil told me some lively stories about Imelda Marcos's attempt to paint, or repaint,

德。我跟他爭論唐吉軻德只是個想像中的人物，不是真的人名，我們的遊戲繼續下去。我剛好帶了兩件 T 恤，打算可以換著穿。兩件剛好都有唐吉軻德印在前面，真是完美的巧合，塞爾尼從開始寫作就很欣賞此書的作者塞萬提斯。他甚至在聖道頓馬士大學的塞萬提斯講座裡描述，塞萬提斯對他的寫作有什麼樣的影響，塞爾尼好幾十年前是從這裡畢業的。這間學校創立於一六一一年，聖道頓馬士大學是亞洲最古老的大學。

往北走的路上，每過一個鎮我們都會在教堂停留拜訪，有些舊的，有些新的。最令人印象深刻是三百多年前西班牙統治時期蓋的教堂。很快的這些教堂跟它們的名字我都記不住了，我的精神信仰消化不良，但是塞爾尼卻把它們變成記憶字典的一部分。但是我記得聖母升天堂，在南伊羅戈省稱聖瑪麗亞教堂，這間教堂非常的雄偉。初建於一七六五年，以磚和灰漿建造，還有一座獨立的鐘樓，一九九三年被聯合國教科文組織認定為世界文化遺產。

塞爾尼對西班牙和美國統治期間跟二次大戰的歷史了解很深，他們對這區域的影響對我來說都是新的知識。塞爾尼指著東邊山上的山口說，這裡曾經有不同的軍隊發生衝突，更別說是最近的新人民軍（*New People's Army*），那是這個國家最大的反政府叛亂組織。

the history of her husband's childhood, recasting him as rising from a higher pedigree in social rank.

Of course the "Wedding of the Century" when their daughter got married in 1983, would not be better forgotten, with an anecdote of mass food poisoning from the special culinary menu prepared and catered to the town from Manila.

Outside a place called The Fort, a casino/resort built by Imelda Marcos, four flags flew side by side; those of the casino, of China, of Taiwan and Hong Kong, a rarity indeed. Politics aside, it may indicate that the most frequent customers must come from those three areas outside of the Philippines.

Without any advance notice, Sionil led me to Vigan, certainly the highlight of this trip. Culture has always been close to my heart, thus CERS while under my watch had conducted numerous culture conservation projects. Yet this UNESCO heritage site is unique, being a largely Spanish colonial town transfixed in time, cast up on the northern coast of the Philippines.

We arrived at dusk. After checking into the Vigan Plaza Hotel in front of the Piazza, we went to dinner at the Leona Restaurant just steps away, adjacent to our hotel. This was not just any restaurant, but a diner which took up the former residence of an important Filipino woman poet/writer. When she wrote her feminist poems and prose she was much ahead of her time, a time

我們在薩拉特（Sarrat）停留，這個城鎮因是馬可仕總統的出生地而出名。我短暫的參觀這間有幾件展示品的屋子。塞爾尼告訴我幾個有關於伊美黛試圖竄改她先生童年的故事，生動有趣，她甚至把他塑造成出生於家世很好的家庭。

當然一九八三年他們女兒的「世紀婚禮」是不可以被遺忘的，有個跟婚禮有關的趣聞。婚禮中的餐點是特別從馬尼拉準備好然後送到這小鎮桌上的，結果吃了這特製食物的賓客很多人都食物中毒。

外面有一個地方叫 The Fort，一間伊美黛馬可仕開的渡假賭場中心，四面國旗掛在一起：賭場的、中國的、台灣的還有香港的，真是個很少見的畫面。撇開政治，這或許告訴我們這裡的常客幾乎是來自這三個菲律賓以外的國家。

在沒有事先告知之下，塞爾尼帶我到維崗，這肯定是這趟旅程他最喜歡的。文化一向都是我最鍾情的，所以 CERS 在我的帶領下主導過很多文化保存的項目。這個聯合國教科文組織認定的文化遺產非常特別，位在菲律賓北方的海岸，一個停留在西班牙殖民時期的小鎮。

我們在傍晚抵達。入住廣場前的維崗廣場飯店後，我們步行到 Leona Restaurant 吃晚飯。這不是間普通的餐廳，這

Inside Santa Maria / 聖瑪麗亞教堂內部

裡以前是一位菲律賓很重要的女性詩人跟作家的家。她
寫的女性主義的詩跟散文在她那年代是前衛的，在那個
年代女性是不被鼓勵甚至被禁止表達自己的思想。正因
如此她被丈夫跟自己的兒子審查、拋棄，最終獨自流亡。

但是這卻沒有阻止利昂娜佛‧洛倫蒂諾（*Leona Florentino*）寫下這首「詛咒的希望」：

What gladness and what joy, are endowed to one who is loved, for truly there is one to share, all his sufferings and his pain.

My fate is dim, my stars so low, perhaps nothing to it can compare, for truly I do not doubt, for presently I suffer so.

For even I did love, the beauty whom I desired, never do I fully realize, that I am worthy of her. Shall I curse the hour, when first I saw the light of day, would it not have been better a thousand times, I had died when I was born.

Would I want to explain, but my tongue remains powerless, for now do I clearly see, to be spurned is my lot. But would it be my greatest joy, to know that it is you I love, for to you do I vow and a promise I make, it's you alone for whom I would lay my life.

when women were not encouraged, or were even prohibited, from expressing their thoughts. So much so that she was abandoned and censored by her own husband and son, and then lived alone in exile.

That however did not deter Leona Florentino from penning the poem, "Blasted Hope":

What gladness and what joy, are endowed to one who is loved, for truly there is one to share, all his sufferings and his pain.

My fate is dim, my stars so low, perhaps nothing to it can compare, for truly I do not doubt, for presently I suffer so.

For even I did love, the beauty whom I desired, never do I fully realize, that I am worthy of her. Shall I curse the hour, when first I saw the light of day, would it not have been better a thousand times, I had died when I was born.

Would I want to explain, but my tongue remains powerless, for now do I clearly see, to be spurned is my lot. But would it be my greatest joy, to know that it is you I love, for to you do I vow and a promise I make, it's you alone for whom I would lay my life.

One citation had it that Leona had Chinese heritage in her blood line,

傳說 Leona 有華人的血統，這相當有可能，因為華人比西班牙人還更早來到維崗。Leona Florentino 的雕像就在廣場入口處前方，雕像正對步行街的主軸線，這條石子鋪的巷道可以通往西班牙殖民區。如果在第一條巷子右轉的話，再往前走兩條街就到了 Nam Chong 學校，一間華人的幼稚園跟小學，在課後教小朋友中文。

旅途的過程塞爾尼不斷展現出他對中國的興趣，他問我好多關於那裡的現狀，特別問到偏遠地方跟那邊的人，像是絲路上的維吾爾族。他早年的時候去過中國很多趟，甚至還跑到很遠的大寨模範公社，但是近年來都沒有再去中國。

他對歷史很有興趣，尤其是複雜的菲律賓近代史，他對中國人還是西班牙人的蔑視常被拿去引用，但總是被斷章取義。明顯的，塞爾尼對中國和西班牙所遺留下的那些是持正面看待的，更別提他很喜愛中國烹飪藝術。但是他厭惡寡頭政治或是壟斷利益的集團，掠奪自己的人民跟國家，更別提近期湧入的中國暴發戶移民。他的朋友圈裡有許多華裔跟西班牙裔，特別是有教養的一群，當然，希望我也算是其中之一。

一度說到我的第一部車是福斯的金龜車，塞爾尼說冷戰時他曾經開金龜車穿越歐洲，包括東歐。他偶爾也會睡在車

certainly a high possibility given that the Chinese were already here in Vigan before the Spanish. Today a statue of Leona Florentino seated on a pedestal takes up the entrance to the main axis of the walking street, a cobbled avenue, into the Spanish settlement. But if one were to turn right on the first side street, two blocks away is the Nam Chong School, a Chinese kindergarten and elementary school that teaches Chinese after regular school hours.

During our trip together, Sionil had shown repeated interest in China when he asked me numerous questions about the situation there, in particular even asking about distant places and people like the Uighur along the Silk Road. He had visited China early on quite extensively, even travelling to the distant model commune of Dazhai, but had not returned to the country recently.

上，那時候他是馬尼拉日報的記者，遊完歐洲後他還把車子運回馬尼拉。我加碼的說我曾在一九七五年到一九七六年開一台福斯的廂型車從加拿大開到南美洲，他回我說他在扶養一個大家庭的時候曾經擁有一台福斯的廂型車好久一段時間。顯然我們的共同點不只有寫作，甚至連我們選的車跟對旅遊的熱愛都是一致的。

不同的是他已經九十幾歲了，但是心理和精神像個充滿活力的年輕人。我跟他說現在的九十歲已經被視為是新的七十歲；已經六十好幾的我，其實才要進入四十歲。所以我們會繼續夢想。

回馬尼拉的路途上我回想我在維崗的經驗，我獨自在日落後跟日出時踏進的小巷弄，都是在觀光客湧入西班牙區前後。一小部分聯合國教科文組織指定世界文化遺產的舊建築物已經被修復了，全部變成精品旅館跟餐廳。所有的商店，意思是賣東西給觀光客的商店，大多都在頹廢的老舊建築物裡，非常急迫的需要整修。看起來這個遺址只是一個門面，後面隱藏著觀光跟商業。

這些建築物的一部分能不能被整修後變成文化用途設施或是藝術住宅呢？一如往常，我覺得我們應該證明這樣是可行的。我靜靜地對自己承諾我們會尋找一間小房子，在我們的能力範圍裡去整修，把它變成可以展示文化的地方，

With his interest in history, in particular the complex contemporary history of the Philippines, his popularly cited disdain for the Chinese and even the Spanish must have been taken out of context. It is obvious that he holds respect for the positive contributions of these heritages, not to mention his love for Chinese culinary art. However, his distaste for the Oligarchy or cartel type, plundering its own people and country, let alone for the more recent influx of Chinese immigrants of the nouveau riche, is quite apparent. Among his circle of friends, there are many of Chinese or Spanish descent, especially those who are principled and disciplined. Certainly I hope I am considered one.

At one point when I mentioned that my first car was a VW Beetle, Sionil said he drove a Beetle throughout Europe, including Eastern Europe, during the Cold War. He occasionally even slept in it while being a reporter for the Manila Times, before he shipped the car back to Manila at the end of his tour of duty. When I upped my ante by saying that I drove a VW van from Canada to South America from 1975 to 1976, he countered that he had a VW van for a long time while raising a large family. Obviously we have more than just a love of writing in common, extending even to our choice of cars and our wanderlust.

The difference is that he is into his 90s, yet with the mind and spirit of an energetic youth. I told him that today 90 is considered the new 70, whereas for myself, while into my late 60s, I am barely into the new 40s. So our

也許是一間畫廊給菲律賓的攝影師做展覽，只展有關於這個國家跟他的人民的作品。這個企圖或許很高，但是我們總是有遠大目標。有些我們實現了，但不是都沒有遇到挫折。

我很榮幸這趟去北菲律賓的短程旅行是由一位熱愛自己國家跟生命的人作為嚮導。塞爾尼不只是個嚮導，他是指路明燈。

House requiring restoration / Repair badly needed ‧ 急需修復的房子

dreams will continue.

While driving back to Manila, I pondered upon my experience in Vigan, the alleys I paced alone in darkness as well as at dawn, before the old Spanish quarters were flooded with tourists. Of the small percentage of old buildings that have been restored in this UNESCO World Heritage Site, all have been turned into boutique hotels and a few restaurants. All other shops, meaning tourist shops, are in largely dilapidated buildings, sorely needing restoration. It seems the heritage designation is only a façade masking tourism and commercialism.

Cannot some of these buildings be restored to become cultural facilities or artistic residences? As usual, I feel we should demonstrate that it can be done. I quietly promise myself that we should look for a small house within our capacity to restore, and turn it into a cultural showcase, perhaps as a gallery for Filipino photographers to exhibit work that focuses strictly on their own country and her people. It may be a high mark of ambition, but we always have lofty goals. Some of them have turned into reality, though not without hurdles.

I feel honored to be guided on this excursion into the distant north of the Philippines by someone who is so passionate about his country, and about life. Sionil is much more than a guide, but a guiding light.

獵頭人不再！

HEAD HUNTER
NO MORE

Dabang Alishan, Taiwan – September 6, 2016

獵頭人不再！

數人頭，越數越少。不過這些並不是真的人頭，在歷史上鄒族會去鄰近敵人那裏獵人頭，而這項傳統已經在大約一世紀前被廢止了。現在數的人頭是鄒族的人口，縮減到只剩不到七千人（也有不到四千的說法）。

「如果再繼續這樣下去，過不了幾個世代我們將會滅族。」戴素雲警告說，她一邊說，一邊仔細地泡著很好的茶給我們喝。我們是來這裡視察鄒族傳統房舍的項目。

戴女士是安達明的夫人，在阿里山達邦這裡是位相當成功的茶農，這裡出產台灣最好的茶葉，也是台灣原住民鄒族的家鄉。戴女士雖然非常擔憂鄒族的未來，但是她本身卻不是鄒族人，她是嫁給鄒族人。這個部落的命運，甚至她老公的後代未來無疑地岌岌可危。

「我們有一個女兒，早就過了適婚年齡，但是她好像一點也不急著結婚。事實上這裡適婚的對象也很少，所以她寧願單身。」戴女士有點沮喪地說。「年輕人不是不結婚，

HEAD HUNTER NO MORE

The heads are being counted, fewer and fewer. But these are not the heads the Tsou people historically hunted when they raided their neighboring enemies. That custom has been abolished and died almost a century ago. It is the head count of their own people, dwindling now to fewer than 7,000 individuals.

"If the current trend continues, our people will be extinct in a few generations." Dai Su-yun sounded her alarm, chatting with me over a fine cup of tea that she carefully brewed for us. We are here to inspect our project among her people.

Dai is the wife of An Da-ming, one of the most successful tea farmers in the Alishan region at Dabang, which is the heart of where the best Taiwan teas are grown, as well as the heart of the indigenous Tsou people of Taiwan. Though Dai is very concerned about the future of the Tsou people, she herself is not of Tsou ancestry, but married into the family. The fate of the tribe, of the ethnic group, and even of her husband, is no doubt in jeopardy.

"We have one daughter, well-passed marrying age, and she seems in no hurry

CERS two Tsou buildings / 兩間鄒族傳統房舍由 CERS 設計搭建

to get married. In fact, there are so few options around here for a mate that she would rather stay single," Dai said with a somewhat sad tone. "Young people either don't marry or, even if married, don't have kids. And many of the younger ones leave here and flock to the city," Dai further lamented.

While sipping her very fine award-winning tea, I promised to ask my close friend Professor Yu Shuenn-der, a leading ethnologist of Taiwan's Academia Sinica, to come and have a look. At the moment, Professor Yu is staying at our Zhongdian Center, continuing his yearly studies of Tibetans at a neighboring village in Yunnan. Perhaps a survey and proper demographic study here would help reveal a bit more about reasons for the grave situation the Tsou people are facing.

"My brother-in-law is a very experienced doctor in reproductive medicine and constantly handles infertility cases. Perhaps he can come and help too," I suggested. "But if the children of the Tsou simply do not want to have babies, then perhaps we need to send in a phycologist or marriage counselor/planner instead," I quickly added.

While much of the world is facing the pressure of population explosion, the Tsou people are in the reverse, trying futilely to be more fertile and grow their numbers, which were small to begin with. Small enough that even Wikipedia only has a six-line entry about the Tsou people, far less than what some of us

要不就是結了也不生小孩。還有很多年輕人離開這裡跑去城市。」戴女士感嘆道。

一邊喝著她的得獎茶，我跟她承諾我會請我的好友余舜德教授來這裡看看，余教授是台灣中央研究院頂尖的民族學者。此刻余教授正在我們的中甸中心繼續他每年對雲南附近藏人村莊的調研。也許調查跟適當的人口研究可以幫助了解現在鄒族陷入的處境。

「我妹夫是個生殖醫學領域相當有經驗的醫生，經常處理不孕的案例。也許他也可以來幫忙。」我建議說，「但是如果鄒族的年輕人單純的不想生，那或許我們需要把心理學家或是婚姻顧問之類的專家找來幫忙。」我很快的補充一句。

Tsou village in the 1920s / Tsou men weaving bamboo．
資料照：1920 年代鄒族村莊 / 正在編竹子的鄒族男人

at CERS know about this unique tribe.

Perhaps that is somewhat understandable. Because of their head-hunting tradition, very few people dared to enter the region in the past. One exception was Torii Ryuzo, a Japanese anthropologist who studied the Tsou around 1920 when Taiwan was still under Japanese occupation. His richly illustrated book recorded the last vestiges of the Tsou tribe and formed the basis of what we now know of as the colorful history and unique practices of this people.

Even up until the mid-1970s, it was difficult to acquire the special permit necessary for any foreigner to enter the region. Some remote villages claim to have seen foreign visitors only once or twice. In 1984, an ageing Japanese anthropologist entered a village and was told that he was only the second foreign visitor, ever. The other was a Japanese woman missionary, over half a century ago.

Tsou tribe and ceremonial house / 資料照：鄒族人與庫巴

當世界上大部分的地方面臨到的是人口爆炸的問題時，鄒族人遇到的確是相反的問題，他們原本的人口就不多，想要增加人口又徒勞無功。少到在維基百科裡只有六行字的描述，太少了，CERS 一些工作人員認識這個獨特民族的知識遠比維基百科上的還多。

這或許也是可以被理解的。因為他們過往的獵人頭傳統習俗，沒有幾個人膽敢進入這區域。唯一一個例外是鳥居龍藏，他是日本人類學家，在一九二零年左右研究鄒族，那時候台灣還是日本的殖民地。他的書圖文並茂地記載著鄒族最後的樣貌，構成我們現在對鄒族認識的基礎，鄒族擁有很豐富的歷史，還有獨特的風俗習慣。

即使到了一九七零年代中期，任何外國人想要取得入山證進去這區域都是非常困難的。有些偏遠村莊聲稱他們只有看過一、兩次外國人。一九八四年一位年老的日本人類學家進入這個區域，村民告訴他，他是來這裡的第二個外國人。另外一位是在半世紀前來這裡的日本女傳教士。

CERS 的項目在達邦，是鄒族社區的中心，小鎮裡人口超過八百人，不到三條街區。其他住民散落在附近的山丘上，山谷裡，大多從事種植茶葉跟其他農業。

五年前一個偶然的機會，透過安孝明（Amo）跟他的夫人

Dabang where CERS has our project is the center of the Tsou community, with over 800 people in the tiny village town, less than three city blocks square. Others spread out over the nearby hills and valleys, mainly conducting tea farming and other agricultural production.

Through a chance meeting five years ago with Amo and his wife Huiling, we got to know better the Tsou culture and its disintegration. The young couple were very keen to find a way to restore to some degree their people's past. Hunting, a mainstay of the Tsou people's traditional activity, had largely been curtailed. The culture that was attached to this subsistence livelihood likewise eclipsed and disappeared. Modern yet simple houses had replaced the indigenous thatched roof houses of the Tsou.

Amo and his wife had been dreaming of rebuilding at least one such house as a testimony to their past. Coming through their simple abode's door was a CERS team exploring the area for the first time. We were impressed by their passion and made a multi-year commitment to assist them in realizing their dreams.

Through several more visits and multiple trips by our Taiwanese designer Sharon Ko and associate Eufung Hwang, the project gradually moved along. Today, two rather impressive buildings have been erected, sitting majestically deep inside a very remote mountain valley of Dabang. There are dormitory, kitchen, bathrooms, dining and even an exhibit area. A third building is being planned.

慧玲讓我們更了解了鄒族的文化和它正在瓦解的狀況。年輕人非常熱切地想要找到方式來保存先人的過去。打獵是鄒族傳統中很重要的活動，但是大多都被禁止。他們賴以維生的打獵活動所衍生出來的文化也隨之黯然失色與消失。現代卻簡單的房屋已經取代了鄒族傳統的茅草屋。

Amo 跟他的夫人夢想著重建至少一間傳統房屋，當作是歷史的見證。走過他們家簡單的大門，CERS 團隊第一次來這裡進行探索。我們對他們的熱情印象深刻，承諾我們會投入幾年的時間來幫助他們完成夢想。

我們台灣的設計師柯詩倫跟學會的工作人員黃毓芳去了好多趟之後，項目開始進行。現在已經有兩棟令人刮目相看的傳統草屋，雄偉地座落在達邦的深山谷地上。裡面有宿舍、廚房、浴室、飯堂以及一個展示區。第三棟現在正在規劃中。

年初開始，Amo 跟慧玲已經招待兩百多位當地鄒族的學

Kitchen / Tsou kids practicing ・「現在屋」的廚房 / 學習傳統技藝的鄒族小孩

Since early this year, Amo and Huiling have hosted over two hundred local Tsou students to visit the premises. These young people not only come to look at the buildings and the collection of Tsou relics inside, but are taught how to use the traditional knife to make utensils, how to use bow and arrows in archery, how to start a fire over a traditional stone stove and cook a simple yet tasty meal. At times, they were invited even to stay overnight in the two houses.

During our own visit recently, we observed with keen interest nine Tsou children, barely ten to twelve years old, enthusiastically spending their Sunday learning to live as their ancestors had done in the past. Yes, this is another small CERS project, again started with little fanfare and visibility, now coming into fruition.

Heading back to "civilization", I left Alishan riding the small-gauge train which was started over a hundred years ago by the Japanese. Along the way I occasionally caught glimpses of the many cars and busloads of people heading up to the famous tourist destination of Alishan. No one would ever take a

Amo teaching archery / Amo 教小孩射箭

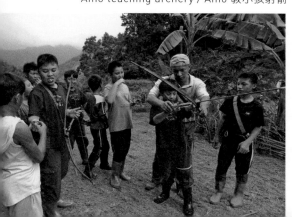

生來這裡參觀。孩子們來這裡不只是來看看建築物跟鄒族的文物而已，他們也來學習怎麼使用傳統的刀來製作器具；怎麼用弓、箭來射箭；怎麼在傳統的石爐上生火煮頓簡單又美味的一餐。有時候他們還會被邀請在這兩棟屋子裡過夜。

最近的這一趟，我們觀察到九位鄒族的小孩，介於十跟十二歲之間，在禮拜天很踴躍地學習他們祖先生活的方式。是的，這又是 CERS 另一個小項目，也是一開始沒有大張旗鼓，跟能見度，但是現在已經可以看到些許成果了。

我坐著一百多年前日本人做的小火車下阿里山，回到「文明社會」。沿途偶爾會見到小客車跟巴士載著人們上到阿里山出名的觀光景點。沒有人會繞道去造訪達邦裡獨特的鄒族人，不過對我來說達邦的大自然和野生生態也是很棒的。

不過究竟有多少人聽過這個這麼小的原住民部落？或許這樣更好。我心裡知道，未來的鄒族人在周末會有一個場所跟祖先有所連結。

也許當他們有了自我認同後，會過得更有尊嚴與自尊。這樣他們也有可能完成另一個新的使命，增加和延續人口，提升這群曾經雄偉、英勇獵頭族的人頭數。

detour to visit this unique Tsou people of Dabang, but for me even the nature and wildlife of Dabang are just as wonderful.

But then, how many people have ever heard of such a small indigenous tribe. That might as well be. I knew in my heart that the future generation of the Tsou people would have a weekend playground where they would feel connected to their ancestors.

Perhaps with their own identity, they will also live with more dignity and integrity. With that, they may also fulfill a new mission, multiplying and perpetuating their population to enhance the headcount of these once majestic and gallant head-hunting people.

國家圖書館出版品預行編目 (CIP) 資料

文化志向 / 黃效文著 .
-- 初版 . -- [新北市]：依揚想亮人文 , 2016.11
面；　公分
ISBN 978-986-93841-1-7（平裝）

855   105019551

文
化
志
向

作者・黃效文 ｜ 發行人・劉鋆 ｜ 責任編輯・王思晴 ｜ 美術編輯・Rene Lo ｜ 法律
顧問・達文西個資暨高科技法律事務所 ｜ 出版社・依揚想亮人文事業有限公司 ｜ 翻
譯 ・ 依揚想亮人文事業有限公司 ｜ 經銷商・聯合發行股份有限公司 ｜ 地址・新北
市新店區寶橋路 235 巷 6 弄 6 號 2 樓 ｜ 電話・02 2917 8022 ｜ 印刷・禹利電子分色
有限公司 ｜ 初版一刷・2016 年 11 月（平裝） ｜ ISBN・978-986-93841-1-7 ｜定價・
400 元 ｜ 版權所有　翻印必究 ｜ Print in Taiwan